365 Days Less 2 Days

by

Austin O'Donovan

Dedicated to the memory of my late father & brother Donal

Designed & Printed by the Limerick Leader.

Forward

Public houses I knew and frequented in Limerick City since the early forties on and off to the present day. One might think the title of my new book is rather strange, until I explain I am actually writing about some of the many experiences I have had in certain public houses during my life. Some of the public houses that I write about are no longer with us, but I feel they should be remembered, it also gives the reader some idea of how far the pubs in Limerick have come in over fifty years or more.

In Ireland most public houses are open for business three hundred and sixty five days in the year, with the exception of leap years. The only days they are legally closed are Good Friday and Christmas Day, hence the title of this book.

I might add most of the public houses that I remember back in the early nineteen forties, would have had sawdust sprinkled on their floors, to protect them from tobacco and pipe smokers spitting on them. A lot of shops but especially butcher shops and public houses in particular had sawdust mixed with wood shavings as a floor covering. Morgan McMahon's timber yard in Mulgrave St. was one of the many places where the sawdust could be collected free of charge for whom ever wanted it.

Contents

Chapter 1
Munster Fair Tavern

The Munster Fair Tavern Bar is situated in the middle of the road at the top of Mulgrave St. it is almost facing the main entrance gate to Mount Saint Lawrence's Cemetery. The road to the left took you to Ballysimon on the way to Tipperary. The road on the right led to Bawnmore and the old road to cork. John Moloney is the son of the original proprietor of this well-established public house in Limerick City. Young John took over when his father retired some years ago.

When you were in the Munster Fair Tavern Bar there was a large window that faced down Mulgrave St. You had a full view of anything coming up that way. It was ideal if you happened to be waiting for a funeral to come up to Mount Saint Lawrence's cemetery. You could see it coming from a long way off.

There was two ways to exit the bar if you wanted to join a funeral procession; one door took you to the fair green side and the other to the graveyard side. It was quite easy to slip into the funeral procession if you didn't like the long walk from the church to the grave. Guys used to get a lift up and have a drink while they waited for the hearse to cross the door, then quietly slip in to the procession.

On horse fair days the Munster Fair bar would be packed with farmers and horse dealers from all over Ireland and as far away as England and France. The farmers coming into town in those days didn't have very much respect for scrubbed floors. Most of the premises would have had a contraption out side their front doors for people to scrape the mud or whatever was stuck on to their boots off.

Just imagine a half dozen farmers coming into your house after standing in cow or horse dung at a fair on a wet and miserable day. It could be worse they may have been coming from the pig market. I don't have to draw a picture for you about the mess pig slurry makes, when it is being dragged around on several pairs of Wellington boots after a fair day.

What you have to bear in mind in those days, horses were used to transport and deliver goods to most shops and premises of one sort or another. People travelled in pony and traps and sidecars, and for a multitude of delivery jobs. Funerals alone going up to Mount Saint Laurence's Cemetery, and the guys that had to walk after the horses, pulling the horse drawn carriages, were a nightmare for the publicans in keeping their floor horse crap free.

As a young lad I was often brought into a public house with my father or one of my uncles or some friend of the family. To my memory, Christenings, First Communions, Confirmations, Weddings, were all happy occasions to visit the local hostelries, in whichever area we happened to be living in at the time. Of course any excuse was used to visit the local public house to enjoy the singsong and have the crack.

There wasn't a day in any year where an excuse couldn't be made for making a visit to the pub. The one and only thing that was required on entering any drinking establishment, was the green backs or in other words money, to buy when it was your turn to buy a round.

Your card would be marked very quickly, if it were thought that you were just there to sponge drink from some poor bloke that had too much to drink.

Little did the clientele that frequented these public houses know that their behaviour was being observed and monitored on an ongoing bases, everyone was secretly getting their card marked. The Proprietor or his wife might happen to say in conversation, "Who was that guy you were talking to". The inquisition may follow, like where does he work, where does he live, where does he come from. Finally you may hear them say do I know any of his people?

It never failed to bring out the whole history of a misfortunate guy, that may have only came into the pub to use the toilet and called for a drink as an excuse. Some bar fly would be only too glad or happy to fill in the details about the mystery man in the bar or using the toilet.

The early morning market bars within sight of St John's Cathedral, in the late forties would have been my first memories of this sort of investigations and interrogations about guys frequenting the local public houses. Market and fair days for a publican could be a nightmare at times. The Fair Green would be swarmed with horse buyers and travellers from wide and far. The Munster Fair Tavern Public house at the top of Mulgrave St. and surrounding area of the Pike and Garryowen was like a Wild West town.

I often remember my grandfather telling me about the squad of corporation workers detailed to go to the fair green to sweep the horse dung off the roads and footpaths, left after the horse fair was over. The best fertilized gardens for growing vegetables were in Bengal Terrace, the pike and Garryowen. The horse manure was also prized and collected in boxes and buckets for flower gardens and especially rose gardens.

The Publicans made a fortune out of the crowds attending those horse fairs. On top of that they had the early morning markets off Cathedral Place. These markets opened from about five o'clock in the morning and went on till the afternoon. Hay, pigs, sheep, and cattle were sold at those markets. Needless to say the local public houses and eating-houses were doing a roaring trade.

They were conveniently dotted around the city adjacent to all the markets that were going on. Hogan's eating house situated on the high street near The Round House public house was the most famous of these eating-houses for strangers coming into Limerick. They were well known for serving up good grub.

One had to be careful drinking in some of those public houses, not to get sick after being served a bad pint of porter. It wasn't unusual for some publican's wife to slip you a pint that was poured from the slop bucket. One or two public houses that I remember being in, with my father, were well known to have sent a few unwanted customers away with a belly ache, a stale pint of porter would keep them sitting on the toilet for a week or more.

Over the years the Munster Fair Tavern public house has been frequented by many famous Limerick men of one sort or another, sometimes they returned home to attend funerals of loved ones, or to live here after living in other countries far and wide for years. One such guy I remember that actually made the Munster Fair Tavern his local public house was a man called Sean Bourke.

He became famous for helping master spy George Blake escape from Wormwood Scrubs Jail in London in 1966, when he himself was serving a term of imprisonment. Sean Bourke wrote a book about his exploits and how he actually helped George Blake achieve this; he could be seen sitting in various bars in Limerick and in the seaside resort of Kilkee. More often than not, at other times he could be seen sitting in the Munster Fair Tavern Bar, looking at the occasional funeral passing him by.

To my knowledge the only life he knew after he became famous and made big money for writing his book, was drinking in public houses in Limerick bars in winter and vacating to Kilkee to do the same thing for the summer Months. Sean Bourke was a nephew of feathery Bourke who I mention in another chapter, Sean Bourke died a young man and is buried in the grave yard beside the public house, where he wrote most of his story about how he set a famous double agent free.

The only thing left to say about the Munster Fair Tavern Bar. It will always do a trade as long as funerals keep passing it's doors, and with Mount Saint Lawrence's present and new extension. Another factor in it's favour is most funerals have to pass that way on their way up to the other new cemetery Mount Saint Oliver's in Bawnmore.

On top of that another plus going for it is, it's only for the last few years to my knowledge that they have been selling draught Guinness. It was a well-known fact that they only sold Murphy's stout on draught. The pub was tied to Murphy's Brewery and it could only sell their product. Of course I'm open for contradiction on that one. Anyone coming out the main gate of Mount Saint Lawrence's cemetery, on a cold miserable rainy day has only to cross the road to enjoy a nice hot whiskey, or brandy and port as I often did.

I have it on good authority that the craic is fairly good in this public house on weekends. I know for a fact that there are great singers frequenting this middle of the road public house. One man in particular known in Limerick as one of the greatest lead plumbers to hold a paraffin oil blow lamp in his hands. His name is Mick Mulcahy you can look into the sitting room of his home from the bar in the Munster Fair Tavern.

Mick is originally a blow in from Kilalee; he left that famous part of Limerick to live with the snobs in St. Laurence's Park. He was Jim Kemmys right hand man and still talks of him as if he was still with us. Unfortunately Jim Kemmy and Kevin Hannon two of our famous historians and writers are no longer with us.

I'm glad to hear that that a lot of the old stock that I knew from Rossa Villas and around Garryowen and the Pike are frequenting The Munster Fair Tavern. Guys like Billy Reeves one of the famous Reeves family of painters in Limerick City, who I might add his brother Danny inspired me to write this book.

Unfortunately Danny is no longer with us, I give him another mention in chapter seven in one of his favourite public houses Maimie Bartlett's Bar. Some of those great tradesmen that I had the pleasure of working with are mentioned in the next chapter of this book

Chapter 2
Brannigan's

Brannigan's public house is situated on Mulgrave St. a few hundreds yards down from The Munster Fair Tavern public house, and was facing Mount Saint Lawrence's cemetery and Saint Joseph's Mental Hospital. This bar was originally known as Molly Ryan's public house, but years later it changed hands to Molly Ryan's sister who was married to a man called Kelly.

The Kelly's ran it for years until it was bought a man by the name of George Newnham who bought it in the early seventies. George once told me he had been a pilot in the Royal Air Force in the First World War. Whatever age George was he didn't show it, he was a tall man with a well-groomed full head of grey hair. He really only bought Kelly Pike Bar as a kind of hobby to be around people. He loved to walk out around his pub and chat to people. He used to be immaculately dressed and always loved to smoke cigars.

I got to know George Newnham shortly after he purchased the pub. He paid thirty-eight thousand pounds for this public house in the early seventies. We were told he sold the Limerick Motor Works for a quarter of a million pounds at the time. George had a very good friend by the name of Pather McNamara who had done bits and pieces of work in Georges house in Castletroy. It seems Pather was a bit of Jack-of-all-trades.

He trusted Pather to take on the big job of renovating the whole public house. Money was no object he was told to employ whatever trades men that was required to carry out the job in hand. The first carpenter he jobbed was my good friend Brendan O'Neill from Garryowen. Brendan came from a great family of carpenters; I had worked with

Brendan and his father Paddy O'Neill in the construction of the new terminal building at Shannon Airport. Sadly Brendan's father died making his way to work one winter's morning. Shortly after that the job came to an end as most building jobs do.

Brendan took his fathers death very hard and went on the beer. We went our separate ways for a while, until one day he called me and asked me if I would fall in with him and work in the renovations of Kelly's Pike Bar. It called for a second carpenter and Brendan gave me first choice. I was delighted the job called for seven days a week with lots of overtime at one pound ten shillings per hour, direct labour it was called each man was responsible for stamping his own insurance cards.

When Brendan and I worked in Shannon the basic rate for a carpenter was twenty-nine pounds ten shillings for a forty-hour week after overtime and working seven days per week we were lucky to take home fifty pounds per week. After that we had to pay the car we travelled in to and from work one pound ten shillings. Compare that to working for George Newnham earning over one hundred pounds per week and he treated us to a few pints of beer every night we finished work. I felt as if all my birthdays were coming together and there was at least six Months left in the job.

We carried out the job to perfection according to the plans. George Newnham's brother was an architect in Dublin he called to see us and discuss his plans for the pub. Pather Mack recruited the heavy gang like ground workers and block layers. Brendan suggested he engage the Electricians, Plumbers, Plasterer's, and Painters from the local talented tradesmen living in the area and drinking in the bar. Pather brought one young lad to work that lived near him in Park.

His name was Gerry McNamara this young man was the strongest and hardest worker I ever saw. Gerry died tragically in Barrington's Hospital. It seems he was drinking to celebrate his twenty-first birthday in the A one Bar on the Dublin Road. Gerry had a habit of bringing a quart bottle of cider home to quench a thirst if he woke up at night.

Unfortunately Gerry mixed up the cider from another quart bottle he had under his bed that contained a weed killer. He drank from the wrong bottle and died roaring in Barrington's Hospital a few hours later. That was such a shock to his poor widowed mother who he lived with in their small vegetable spread in park. It affected the whole gang so much that after his funeral we all went on the batter for over a week.

All the gang that worked on the renovations that we carried out in the public house were treated to a huge piss up by George Newnham, Food and drink were laid on in abundance. Everyone got a special bonus in his wage packet on top of that. The whole of Garryowen and the Fair green attended the function and to see the work that we done in the public house. The extension that was built on to the lounge bar was huge. George Newnham got a big office beside his huge storeroom and there was an office for his bar manager Ted Halvey.

A separate poolroom was built off the public bar, and another entrance was opened leading in from the Garryowen Road side of the Pike. The ladies and gents toilets that were newly rebuilt were out of this world. A new kitchen was built to accommodate the food end of the business. The best team of workers I ever had the pleasure of working with were engaged in doing that job.

Another day I was in the front public bar as it was called then playing card for turkeys, it was around Christmas time. Jim Madden one of our friends and one of the plumbers engaged in the renovations in the public house went up to the bar to get a round of drink. The bar was packed and the crowd were standing shoulder to shoulder to try and reach the bar. As it happened a big strong man with wide shoulders was blocking Jim's way.

Jim had a few pints in him and thought by tipping your man in the shoulder he would move out of his way. When the guy turned around he had a face that one would have imagined, had gone twenty rounds in the ring with Mike Tyson. His nose was flattened sideways against his cheekbone and appeared to be facing in the direction of his right ear. All poor Jim could do was say he was sorry and turned away towards the guys playing cards at the card table.

What made me laugh was, Jim put his finger up and flattened his own nose, to imitate the big guy standing at the counter. Then passed this remark saying, "Your man's trouble was he didn't get enough of the tit from his mother when she was breast-feeding him". Well if the poor guy had heard what Jim was after saying about him, he would have wrecked the place.

Some of them are no longer with us, and I feel I should mention who they were just for the record. George Newnham paymaster, Pather McNamara the gaffer, Mick Bevel block layer, Jackie O'Shea plasterer, Tommy Anslow wall and floor tiller, Jim

Madden and Mick Mulcahy plumbers, Billy Reeves painter and decorator, Connie Howard and Jimmy Mulcahy cabinet makers, Ramey Mulqueen and Gerry McNamara General operatives, and of course Brendan O'Neill and myself. The electrical work and the carpet-layers were done by outside contractors.

My thanks goes out to the bar manager at that time Ted Halvey, and his fleet of male and female staff who looked after all the workers supplying drink to all on the orders of George Newnham, so much for Kelly's Pike Bar I hope we all meet again in Heaven. For my last words I wish the people of Garryowen and the Pike well, and all who frequent this public house under the new management of Brannigan's.

Chapter 3

Jerry O'Deas Bar

Jerry O'Deas Bar is situated in Mulgrave St. and it is beside the Limerick prison; it is facing O'Donovan Rossa Avenue, otherwise known as Congress Avenue. This terrace of houses was opened in 1932 the year of the Eucharistic Congress. That year was a big year in the Catholic Church calendar, the Pope of Rome sent his delegate Cardinal Von Rossium to attend this great event in Dublin. Every street in every village and town and city in Ireland had their houses decorated with Holy pictures, Papal flags, and bunting of all colours on display outside their houses. The Mass was broadcast and all the proceeding that took place on that day in the Phoenix Park in Dublin, was blurted out loud on every wireless at the time in the country.

Shaw's meat factory later known as Clover Meats was at the other side of Jerry O'Deas bar. On dog racing nights this huge bar would be packed to capacity. They did a huge passing trade also. Funerals alone in my opinion going up Mulgrave St. could keep this public house going, crowds always seemed to congregate in Gerry's bar after funerals.

The front bar was capable of holding a large crowd, but when you went through to the back lounge bar there is large function room in this area as well. Jerry O'Dea as I remember him was a very efficient man behind the bar. I had a friend who worked as a panel beater in Hayes's Garage across the road from the pub. His name was Paddy Bourke he often nipped in to have a drink in Gerry's bar, and spoke nothing but praise for Gerry and all his bar staff. I found that out for myself many a time I was in there after funerals. After funerals Jerry O'Deas bar always seemed to draw a big crowd in.

The back room lounge bar is ideal to cater for families and friends after a funeral has taken place. The grub couldn't be faulted either, there is nothing like tucking into finger licking bar food after having a couple of drinks and having a chat and paying your respects after attending a funeral. The first thing that catches your eye in the back room lounge bar in Jerry's, apart from the very comfortable seating accommodation, is the silver cups and trophies encased in glass cases.

Greyhounds that belonged to Gerry's uncle John Joe O'Dea won those trophies.
I remember being in London in 1953 and being told by my uncle that a Limerick dog owned by John Joe O'Dea the publican had won the puppy derby in the White City stadium in London the year was either 1953 or 54. That would have been a huge success in those days; the name of the dog was Jerry's Clipper. Is it any wonder that the doggy men that attend the dog track week in and out, from all parts of Ireland, make their way to this famous public house in Limerick just a stone throw away from the Markets Field greyhound racing track.

Those racing trophies never failed to be the cause of very interesting conversations about passed achievements of great greyhounds that ran in their day in the Markets Field track. I remember as a child when I lived in Sarsfield Avenue Garryowen, making a few bob minding farmers motorcars when they brought their dogs to race in the track. If their dog won or put any kind of a good show you could be sure of getting a good tip. I often made ten or fifteen shillings minding cars on dog nights.

The ordinary punters were good to tip also the hardest part for me was trying to get around to all the cars to collect your reward as they came out of the dog track. Parked cars would take up every inch of space, and it could be a nightmare for guys to try and get away when the dogs were over. Most guys knew where Jerry O'Deas pub was and would make for there until the rush was over. I still had to wait for them to come back to collect their car and to get paid. Sometimes the tip was good sometimes not so good.

Listening to tales about hard luck stories could be funny at times. I remember being told a story about this guy that had a dog running one night in the Markets Field in one of the heats. He convinced the whole of Cleeve's Condensed Milk factory that his dog was a certainty to win his heat. So much so that a huge crowd from the factory paid to go in and have a bet and see the dog win. The electric hare started and the dogs were barking in the kennels raring to go. As soon as the traps opened the dogs burst out and the (tipped dog), was about six lengths in front, before they came to the first bend. He was travelling so fast he nearly caught the electric hare, and couldn't seem to get around the first bend. Suddenly disaster struck the dog ran straight into the fence, he was lucky he wasn't killed, but his race was all over for that night.

The Cleeve's factory punters that lost their hard earned money were very disappointed. So much so that one disgruntled old guy approached the broken-hearted greyhound owner and fellow worker to offer a bit of advice. He proceeded to tell your man, "If he put a small bit of lead on the dogs left ear it might help him to get around the bend next time". Poor man looked at him and said, "and how could I do that". "With a f****** double barrel shot gun, what did you think said your man?

You couldn't visit Gerry O'Deas public house in those days without hearing jokes of one sort or another. There was a great crown of characters working in Shaw's bacon factory next door to the pub. Some guys didn't go home for dinner hour from one to two, they preferred to have a pint in Jerry's bar and back a few horses across the road in the bookie office. All the pork butchers that I knew would have no trouble sinking a few a pints of Guinness during their dinner hour.

The Siren would go off four times a day for the Shaw's workers early morning calling the work force to work, one o'clock to go to dinner two o'clock to come back and five o'clock to finish in the evening. Each factory had it's own siren and each one was easily recognizable. The loudest one that I can remember was Tate's clothing factory. Each of the many sirens in all the factories in Limerick City and what ever foreign boats that were in the docks, would sound off their sirens from midnight on the 31st December ringing in the New Year, that old tradition has long since gone.

Chapter 4
McLysaghts Bar

McLysaghts public house is situated in Mulgrave St, a few doors down from Gerry O'Deas Bar, on the opposite side of the road and it was facing Morgan McMahon's timber yard. Two brothers ran this small public house; I do remember having a drink in it on a few occasions. The d cor inside needed a lot to be desired, everything about it was far from comfortable. The rungs on the bar stools had seen better days, worn away from farmer's hob nail boots resting on them. They were anything but comfortable to sit on, if you happened to be sitting without your back up against the couple of partitions, put there to support the counter rather than one of the customers drinking at the bar.

McLysaghts did a good trade when De Coursey the auctioneer held his bull sales in the Market quite near the pub. They always managed to fill his small pub with a crowd of farmers on market days. They also had their own regular clientele from the surrounding areas as nearly every pub did. Most of the guys I knew going in there were on the book. Drink away, till pay day, that was the motto, another reason for making that place your local was you could stay there till all hours at night, and on into the early hours of the morning.

In later years when the brothers got old they were very choosey whom they left in to their premises, the front door was always kept locked. The last time I drank in that public house when the McLysaght brothers had it, I was with my friend Brendan O'Neill. He told me to say nothing until the door was opened. Then he proceeded to use the special knock. After a time the bolt on the door was pulled back and one side of the two-sided door was opened. Brendan walked in and I followed. The whole bar was in darkness only for the bit of daylight coming from the kitchen window just off of the bar, at the back of the house.

Brendan asked me what I wanted to drink; I thought to myself for a while and said a pint of Bulmers Cider. He called for two pints of cider hoping he would fill them out of the one quart bottle of cider. His prayers were answered the quart bottle was put up on the counter; we were given two half-pint glasses to fill them as we wanted to ourselves. That cost two shillings and sixpence, or a half crown as it was called; if we were Americans, it would have been half a dollar.

When my eyes got acclimatized to the darkness I recognized another couple of carpenters in the corner that I had worked with from time to time. They were drinking pints of Guinness and it looked good. I gave the nod to Brendan and said we will try a couple of pints after we drink the cider. The one thing we both didn't want was a dicey pint that would give you a dose of the trots. Every time I think of a bad pint I think of Ma O'Leary's bar, which I cover in detail in another chapter.

The McLysaght brothers were very old fashioned in their ways. I don't ever remember a woman serving inside the bar as long as I was going in there. The only time I frequented the place was to meet one of my fellow carpenters in any case. I remember on one occasion I called to collect a friend of mine, for the purpose of this chapter I will call him Scalder and had a drink with him before we left to travel to Clonmel one Friday night.

I was working for a man by the name of James McMahon one of the timber McMahon's, and I subcontracted a bit of work from him that had to be done over the weekend. It meant staying in a bed and breakfast on Friday and Saturday night in Clonmel in Tipperary, James McMahon subcontracted the original work from Creedon's of Dublin, they were big suppliers of suspended ceilings, and partitions, and suspended ceiling contractors in Ireland. I worked on many of their contracts all around Munster, the biggest being Marino Point in Cork. I chose Scalder to work with me because he asked me to give him a turn at making a few shillings for Christmas that wasn't very far off.

I had a whiskey and water while Scalder finished his pint of Guinness; we both joined my boss James McMahon who wouldn't come into the pub. The fact that I had to knock on the door to get in must have put him off. Scalder had a bag packed for our two-night stay like I told him too. McMahon put the boot down and we were in Clonmel in no time. He had arrangements for us to stay in Johnny Murtha's Public house in Clonmel; four pounds each per night was the cost of the B&B.

McMahon wrote a cheque to cover that and wrote two cheques more one for Scalder and one for me. The total amount for our job was one hundred pounds; I decided to split it down the middle with Scalder, and I expected him to give me a good hand so we could both finish it as soon as possible, and get back home on our own steam. In other words we had to get a train or bus home and pay for it ourselves.

McMahon left for Limerick and said he would call back on the Monday, to collect whatever tools needed to be brought home, and whatever materials that was left. Scalder and I inspected the room we were to sleep in for the next two nights. The room was nothing to write home about, just enough room for two single beds. The scenery looking out the back room window was a red-bricked wall that had seen better days; even Scalder said it could do with a bit of pointing.

I took Scalder down to have a quick look at the job in hand. The total square area to be covered was about one hundred square yards. I figured if we made an early start on the Saturday morning, two good men that knew what they were doing could do it in twelve hours. If the worst came to the worse we had Sunday to finish it. Once the levels were marked out at the required height using a water level, which I used, and the angle trim was fixed to the lines we made with the chalk line.

Then the hard part started, holes, had to be drilled in the concrete at four feet centres, toggle bolts were driven in and pulled down with our claw hammers, to spread the wedges, these toggle bolts had a hole in them to suspend a wire from it. The wires were straightened with an electric drill and cut to size, they were left dangling from the concrete ceiling, to receive the carrying channels that supported the weight of the suspended ceiling.

When you reached that stage the tracks were clipped on and it was ready to set it out for receiving the ceiling tiles. I had the experience of putting up thousands of acres of ceilings in my time, and had it off to a fine art. All I needed was a guy to do what I told him. Scalder would have his chance when we came to start this job the next morning. We retired to Johnny Murtha's public house to have a few drinks before we went to bed.

Scalder was well able to speak up for himself when he was in a public house. The barman that served us filled two pints of larger with two big frothy heads on them, and placed them on the counter before us. Scalder looked at them then looked at me and I looked at him. He then asked the barman if he could put a dash of lime into them. When the barman said yes, Scalder attacked and said why didn't you fill them up in the first place instead of giving short measures? Needless to say that remark didn't go down well for the duration of our stay in the B&B in that public house.

My biggest problem was trying to get Scalder up to bed; he wanted one for the road after every other one for the road. Finally when he did manage to finish he suggested we go for fish and chips. That was all right until we walked to the chipper a few doors down from the pub. He found out that they sold pigs toes, and even I came to life again at the prospect of eating a feed of pig's toes, after having a feed of drink. We got two each and forgot about the chips. We made our way back to the B&B and sat on our beds.

A newspaper was spread on the flood to hold the bones that we sucked clean. I suddenly remembered telling Scalder that I was once told that there were sixty-four bones in one pig's toe, or crubeen as they were sometimes called. When the last bone was picked clean, and dropped on the pile that were after creating on the floor. It was time to pay a visit to the bathroom to wash our sticky face and hands. Then we hit the sack; Scalder pulled the cord hanging from the ceiling that plunged the whole room into darkness.

Scalder woke me the next morning coughing and gawking in the bathroom. He had got up to relieve himself and when he found himself in a strange room, and his eyes weren't fully awake, he thought the pile of bones that was between the two beds on the floor, was where I was after getting sick. Scalder always had a very poor constitution, I once saw him to get sick after standing on dog shit.

We managed to get a bit of breakfast down before facing the job ahead. I knew if we gave ourselves a chance we would work off the nights drink and we should be all right after the ten o'clock tea break. Everything went well according to my plans until about four o'clock that afternoon. Then Scalder asked, "if I wanted anything from the shop", "I said no". He said, "he wanted to go into town to buy a scout knife for his son for Christmas". I was well under way, filling in the tiles in the ceiling, so I asked him to open up enough boxes and put them up on the scaffolding until he came back.

Off he went, I didn't see him again for about three hours, and when I did he was well pissed. I told him to go home that he was a danger to himself and struggled on to try and finish. But I knew that there wasn't a hope in hell of finishing it that day, he blew his chance when he left me early in the afternoon. It was nearly time for me to pack up, as the light wasn't great for me trying to cut border tiles while standing on the scaffolding. I was relying on Scalder to have done that and hand them to me.

The rest of that night he spent apologizing to me for what was after happening. I told him for what work was left to be done in the job it was hardly worth his while staying around, and if he wanted to go home he could. He begged me to leave him stay and Scalder swore it would never happen again. There was no feed of liquor or pig's toes that Saturday night, all I wanted to do was get out of Clonmel as soon as possible the next morning.

I was working in Riddler's public house all that week and went straight to Clonmel to oblige Scalder to earn a few extra quid. I knew I was knackered every bone in my body was aching from jumping up and down on the scaffolding. I couldn't wait for to get on the bus home to Limerick. I spoke very little to Scalder after that, when the bus came in the Ballysimon Road to Mulgrave St. He asked to get off outside McLysaghts public house.

I gave him the cheque that he didn't deserve; he thanked me and then went into the bar where I had picked him up. I never worked with him again after that day, and swore I never would. There isn't very much more I have to say about McLysaghts public house that I knew all those years ago. Only to say it's under new management and has been given a complete face-lift.

I'm assured all are welcome, I'm also sure that the nice people of Garryowen, the Pike, and Fair Green, still support all the local public houses in the area, as did their fathers and grandfathers before them. The markets as I knew them are long since gone, but not the descendants of the people that kept them going. Long may it be that way, "Up Garryowen and Glory".

Chapter 5
Cahill's Bar

Cahill's public house is situated in Mulgrave St. and it is beside McLysaghts bar. My first time entering this establishment was back in 1970, the reason I was drawn to this bar was the music and sing song that used to be on at weekends, was just terrific. The bar in those days was run by a sister and brother team Joe Cahill and his sister Brenda. The bar was much larger than McLysaghts bar next door. There were doors that could be folded back opening up the lounge to twice the size.

Cahill's public house made a fortune out of the farmers attending the bull sales in the market behind the bar. It was a fine bright and very comfortable bar to enjoy a drink it. It was one of the few bars around at the time that made sandwiches and sold them. To my knowledge they had a microwave oven when no other public house had one. I for one was amazed to see he hot whiskeys and other beverages made in the microwave oven, in a couple of minutes.

Quite a lot of pork butchers made Cahill's there local public house. I was in there one day and I overheard a butcher asking a farmer how many sets of teeth had a cow? The farmer said "Two I suppose". The butcher said to him, "What kind of a farmer are you? He then went on to explain to the farmer that a cow has only one set of teeth. He went on to tell the farmer that a cow would die where a sheep would live. The reason being that the grass has to be high for the cow to tear it from the ground between his tongue and his upper molars. The sheep on the other hand has two sets of teeth and can crop it almost to the roots.

For once the butcher educated the farmer and it later transpired that a lot of farmers didn't know that. Another thing I learned that day was that a cow and a camel walk the same way, their two legs move the same way, for instance the front left leg and the back hind leg move at the same time, likewise the right fore and hind leg move together. It's amazing the things one hears in public houses at times.

Cahill's pub had quite a lot going for it at the time. Card games were played on a regular basis on the tables around the fire end of the lounge bar. That is of course if you could get anywhere near the fire, as Joe always had barrels taking pride of place around it trying to keep them warm, no one liked to drink cold Guinness especially in the winter time.

Big crowds came to watch the dart throwers in action. Cahill's always had a good dart team representing them. Before the dart board game became popular, throwing rubber rings at the ring board was the in thing. For my part I used Cahill's to listen to the music and the good singers that used to entertain us. My wife and I went as often as we could at weekends.

One man that used to play the accordion was Willie Harris, I knew Willie when he played in Earl Connolly's band in the Stella Ballroom in Shannon St. Willie could nearly make his accordion talk he was so good. I could listen to him all knight playing his lovely selection of all the popular tunes of the day. He wasn't bad at singing them either. As the night drew on about the last hour he would ask for singers to sing, that's when the local talent could show what they could do.

Quite a few very good bar men worked in Cahill's from time to time. Tony O'Connor my favourite barman in my local public house W.J. South's. Which I speak about in another chapter was one, and Donal Duggan the bookmaker worked there at one time, and went on to own three or four bookie offices in Limerick and Tipperary. He sold one to Ladbrokes the big English bookmaking firm, and made a fortune out of it.

Speaking of fortunes Joe Cahill the proprietor and his wife and daughter, and sister Brenda were four of a syndicate of ten that won the Irish Lotto draw in Cahill's public house. They shared a half a million pounds between the ten of them. The sad story about that was, one of the men that were in the syndicate in the pub pulled out only one week before. Needless to say he never got over that, but to my knowledge the rest of the syndicate may have given him some little bit of the winnings as a consolation prize. The old saying goes, "If you're not in you can't expect to win", as your man found out to his cost.

A lot of changes have taken place since the farmer's used to attend the bull auctions in the market at the back of Cahill's public house. Every inch of space has been built on the grounds of the old market. A new headquarters and depot for Limerick Fire Brigade has been built on the Mulgrave St. of the old market. The market area itself was developed and the most beautiful town houses were built there.

That should be good news for the local public houses in the area, there are thousands of people living around that part of town since all the old lanes and every small piece of waste ground was developed since I was a child running around that part of Limerick over sixty years ago. I remember a time when train wagons full of cattle were pushed across the main road in Mulgrave St. and over the Roxboro Road to be loaded on to trains for different destinations all over Ireland.

Other wagons loaded with pigs and sheep were pushed into Shaw's meat factory to be slaughtered. Shaw's were big employers of women and men in those days. There was a certain kind of buzz around the markets in those days; it used to give me the feeling of something special was going on. The first time I ever witnessed a cow giving birth to a calf was in the Haymarket, at the back of Cahill's public house. It's a sight I will never forget as long as I live, and gives some idea of what I mean by a certain buzz.

On the subject of giving birth when the condom machines were first installed in hotels and public house in Ireland. There were plenty of jokes going around in Limerick City, especially in the public houses. One that comes to mind describes a scene that is supposed to have taken place in a public house toilet, not this particular one I might add, where two friends were out for a bit of enjoyment and were trying to get condoms out of the condom machine for the first time.

The first guy read all the instructions that he could see then put his money in the machine and took out one. He had a bit of a hard on so he thought for the crack he would try it on. He felt good and was boasting to his mate. His mate went to the condom machine and bought two and proceeded to put them on, one after the other. "What do you want two on for said his mate, you never know "To be sure" "To be sure, I suppose said your man".

Chapter 6
Horse & Hound Bar

The Horse and hound bar is situated on the corner of Cathedral Place, and Mulgrave St. it is probably one of the best-known market bars in that area, because no matter what side of the market gates you went in or came out you couldn't help but notice it. It was owned by a veterinary surgeon by the name of Mulcahy. I have no doubt the reason he bought it was, if he wasn't doing a good business in the pub, he could fall back on his skills as a vet, with all the animals coming and going from the markets.

The horse and hound was the first public houses I can ever remember to get a complete face lift from the outside to the inside away from the drab looking old public houses that were only held together by the drab paint jobs they were given. It was one of the most modern public houses for its time in the late forties that I can remember. The plasterers can be proud of the job they done to the front and side of this fine bright public house.

To my knowledge it was always painted snow white, the name over the door was a talking point also. Some people used to call it the three-shilling bar, because the half a crown in those days was worth two shillings and sixpence, and it had a horse on the face of it. The sixpence piece had a greyhound on it, put the two together and you had three shillings. I often frequented this public house especially after funerals if the ones up the road nearer to the cemetery were to full.

The horse and hound is now under new management and has been for a good many years. The new proprietor had a butchers shop further down in upper William St. His name is Nichols he married a girl Bernie O'Connor from Knock Na Goshel in county Kerry. I once knew his wife from my visits to the Square Bar, which I cover in another chapter. She had a sister a cheese maker that worked in Cleeve's factory that married another publican called Mossy Kirby he was a brother of Mary Kirby who now owns the Square Bar.

The Horse and Hound was a great place to go for a good breakfast early in the morning, and I mean early anytime after six thirty in the morning. Droves of people made their way to have an early breakfast after coming off night work from Krupps and Ferenka factories. Others had their breakfast before going to work; you could get the smell of the bacon frying a mile away.

The dinners were excellent and all the meat that was cooked came from the proprietor's own shop. He never had to advertise his grub good news travels fast was his motto. The front part of the bar is bright and spacious; the back is cosy and comfortable also. Like most of the pubs around every one had their own clients frequenting them the Horse and Hound was no exception.

I remember when the Ceili dances were going full swing in Saint Johns Pavilion, you wouldn't get standing room with the crowds of men going in there for a drink to try and get a bit of false courage to ask a girl up to dance. The bicycles would be five deep going from the dance hall door up to Morgan McMahon's timber yard. Each mans bicycle would be carrying a girl home on the bar at the end of the night.

The price of the dance on a Sunday night was two shillings, I often came out of that place and my shirt would be stuck to my back. It was a sweatshop if ever there was one, but having said that I wouldn't have changed it for the world. Some of the best times in my life were spent in that dance hall doing the walls of Limerick and the Siege of Ennis. The Stella Ballroom was the place to go if you wanted more and civilized dancing. The pace was much slower than the Ceili dancing, and a lot less rough on you.

I often wondered how the dance floor held up with the hob nailed boots that some farmers wore pounding the floor. Or the skid marks they made wearing Wellington boots. Other guys wore bicycle clips to tie their trouser leg, as some of the suits they wore had twenty-two inch bottoms. Every time they moved around the floor the legs of their trousers would swing around and get tangled in the girl's legs and nearly trip them over.

It was priceless to observe some of those guys standing up at the end of the dance hall. They were all smoking and dangling the cigarettes behind their backs every now and again flicking off the ash from the fags. Some guys were very young but tried to look older. The hair oil would be running down the back of their heads. The plastic ties they wore with the ready-made knots held around their necks with elastic, were some sight to see.

Eventually when they made up their mind to ask a girl to dance, I often felt sorry for the guy that was just robbed from getting a girl to dance with him, just because he was a bit slow crossing over the floor, he had to crawl back to where he was standing and try and build up enough courage to try again. There is a lot to be said for bringing your own girl to the dance. At least you don't have to put up with the humiliation of being refused.

There is nothing like Ceili dancing to get the blood pumping especially if you are caught up in a dance like the siege of Ennis. The thrill of a big strong woman taking hold of you and swinging around like you were some kind of a rag doll is an experience not to be missed. Some women could be right bitches for refusing to dance when they were asked. The dance bandleader would be constantly telling the girls how hurtful it could be for them to refuse to dance with a guy.

The Horse and Hound Bar could be a great place to go to drown you sorrows if you had a bad experience of being refused a dance in Saint Johns Pavilion. You had a chance to take the pledge in Saint Johns Temperance just around the corner from the dance hall, if the reason you were refused was because the girl smelt drink from you. Personally I would take the first option and go to the pub or bring your own girl to the dance as I always did.

Many a time a guy would ask a beautiful girl up to dance, smelling of drink only to be put off and to be told, "I need a smoke, would you ask my sister please, I'm dancing since I came in and I'm sweating". A reply like that would send you back to the pub to try and forget all about dancing. I believe it was the cause of a great number of bachelors being left on the shelf in Ireland in those days also.

Chapter 7
Maimie Barlett's Bar

As you walked from Mulgrave St. up Cathedral Place, in the direction of St. Johns Cathedral, Maimie Bartlett's Public house was the first pub on the left hand side. From what I'm told the licence has since been sold and the pub as I knew it is no more. Maimie Bartlett was an old woman and enjoyed the company of her regular customers more than she did making money. She had her regular customers and most of those got the drink from her at a reduced rate. Most of those regular customers were also on the book. That meant no money passed over the counter for drink until payday usually Thursday or Friday. All drinks were entered in the bar book, you could drink away until payday.

That was the way in most public houses in those times. Some strangers often pulled Maimie if she filled a pint with an exceptional large head on it saying they were getting a short measure. Her regular clients would back Maimie up by saying, "It was a Bishops head pint they were getting" the disgruntled customer might say back, "Well she should think about filling ones with Priests collars on them instead".

One man in particular that I have to mention and I'm sad to say is no longer with us, is Danny Reeves, for some reason unknown to me had the nickname "Fog". He always took Maimie's part and she relied on him a lot. Danny was a painter by trade, and he lived on the Garryowen Road, only a stone throw away from where I lived and who was a personal friend of our family. He is the man that inspired me to write this book. I remember him saying to me and all my friends that frequented so many of the local public houses around our area of Garryowen. "One day I will write a book"?

Danny Reeves loved to go fishing and shooting in Plassey and was a very good angler; the stories he told of the ones that got away were priceless. Another famous boast that Danny often came out with was when a Falcon nested in the Cathedral Tower. It seemed that quite a lot of people from Garryowen were having trouble with the Falcon killing their chickens.

Danny's talents for shooting were called for; he used to say his mother called him out to do something about it. He is reported to have taken his twenty-two Winchester rifle out to his back yard, which was directly at the back of St. Johns Convent School and also behind the Cathedral Tower. In his own words Danny said, "When he got the chicken thief in his sights, he had no chance, all you could see after Danny squeezed the tricker was skin and feathers flying".

Danny Reeves used to say; "If ever he was going to write a book it would be about the goings on he witnessed in public houses, for the three hundred and sixty five days of every year, which is the title I gave my book thanks again Danny, for your inspiration.

Maimie Bartlett loved Danny Reeves and all her faithful and regular customers; she looked forward to seeing them come into her public house. Any friend of her regular customers was always welcomed in her premises. There was never a dull moment when you were in Maimie Bartlett's bar. I don't ever remember visiting her bar without splitting my sides laughing. The clientele that frequented her establishment should have taken up stage work as comedians.

I remember a guy that pawned his suit of clothes to get money until he got paid in the Labour Exchange. He came into Maimie's for a pint; he was wearing an overcoat that came down well below his knees. It's only when he sat down that you could see he had no trousers on.

He was wearing the bottom legs of the only pair of trousers that had been burned while drying them at the fire. They were so badly burned that all he could salvage were the legs from the knee down. In order to make his way to Patie Browns Pawn office, he got a brain wave, he decided to pin what was left of his trouser legs to the inside of his over coat.

To hear him telling how he stepped into them then buttoned up his coat. Making sure he said, "To have a good shine on his shoes before doing so". That he said, "Done the trick", when he stood up you would swear he was wearing a suit.

He finished up by saying that after he had drank his pint, he was going to chance going over to the Dispensary to get a docket for a new pair of trousers. Needless to say we were all in stitches laughing. But as it happened when the word got out about his circumstances someone offered him clothes belonging to a relative that had died.

I was in there another time and I overheard a guy saying to his friend that he couldn't afford to buy a drink. He said that all he had in his pocket was the price of a Mass card he wanted to put on a neighbours coffin, and the five shillings to get it signed by one of the Priests in Saint Johns Cathedral.

How's your father said to him, "Go out to the shop and bye the Mass card and I will sign it? Than you will be able to buy one pint for me and have three for yourself. You can have the mass said another time for the guy in the coffin".

I can't leave this public house without mentioning a very special friend of mine whose family would have used this public house on a regular basis. His name is Brendan O'Neill, Brendan's father Paddy and his brothers all very good carpenters would have known all the lads that I have mentioned in this chapter very well.

The fact that most of the guys drinking in this public house at the time were living in Cathedral Place, or Brennan's Row. A lot of them came from Kilalee or Garryowen may have had something to do with it also. As I already said the guys frequenting these early morning houses were great tradesmen.

I knew another character that was a pork butcher whose nickname for the purpose of telling this joke was called the Devil. He is said to have visited his Doctor ailing with some complaint or other. The Doctor gave him a prescription to get a bottle in the form of a rub; it was to be rubbed into the skin. The Devils sight wasn't great, and he had a bad memory and couldn't remember what the Doctor said to him, he couldn't make out the instructions on the bottle, so he decided to drink it, much to his regret afterwards. He wound up being taken to Barrington's hospital to be pumped out.

The Devil was a hard man in his day; the stories that went around about him if you could believe them were unreal. The Devil was also a great character the sayings he used to come out with were priceless. He had spent some time in America back in the days when prohibition was the order of the day. His favourite song was "Buddy can you spare a dime". He often spoke about his time living in America, and the gangsters he said he knew. The Devil was a pork butcher by trade, and for some reason the word spread in the Bronx but got mixed up in the slang.

The Devil got the reputation that he had to leave Ireland over the amount of pigs he killed. To kill a pig in the states meant a Policeman, to kill one in Ireland meant a "Porky". Casual workers in the bacon factories in Limerick in those times were called "yanks", I never did know why. But I do know a lot of Irishmen emigrated to America. Most that went over stayed and were conscripted to do military service, and found themselves back in Europe fighting the Germans in the Second World War. I suppose the guys that were taken on to replace those guys that went to America, got the name temporary "Yanks".

Anyone just listening to the conversations going on between

the regular customers couldn't help but be educated. For instance when the bird fanciers were in the bar nothing else interested them only to talk birds. Most of those men were experts and had a great knowledge of all kinds of birds. Some of the Garryowen men were very skilled at making different kinds of birdcages; some bred their own birds. There was a pet shop in Gerald Griffin Street, beside the basket maker. He bought birds and cages from the birdmen in Garryowen. Some other men specialized in catching wild birds they had different methods of doing that.

One way was to bring a good singing bird in a cage, to an area in the quarry to act as a lure, to draw wild birds to the net traps. These traps were bated with bread or birdseed ready to pull when the unsuspecting birds were eating. Other more cruel ways were used like putting birdlime on the branches of trees that the birds used. This stuff was sticky and held the bird to the branch. I was told birds caught this way didn't live very long; the glue did a lot of damage to their legs and feathers. Real bird fanciers would never approve of catching wild birds in that way.

I personally knew several guys that kept racing pigeons around the locality. Big money changed hands for pigeons, some were sent to Dublin and Belfast on the train to be released and timed when they came home. The more ambitious guys sent them as far away as England and France. All those pigeon fanciers would meet up in the quarry at one time or another and the conversation was all about every kind of pigeon, from homing, to racing, to tumbling pigeons.

You would hear great stories about pigeons being used to deliver very important messages during the War. The thousands of miles they travelled and about the hawks that were sent up to try and kill them. Some stories I'm sure were made up but it was great to hear a fellow telling them.

Chapter 8
The Moose Bar and How's Your Father

The Moose Bar is situated in Cathedral Place, and has been in the Tobin family for years, and still is; it was the next pub up from Maimie Bartlett's it was on the corner of Cathedral Place, and Smiths Row. This public house was another glue pot to get out of. Being a market bar it opened around five o'clock every morning, except Sundays. The characters that frequented that bar were priceless. My own Uncle was one of them. He had a saying when greeting anyone, he usually greeted anyone he met by saying, "How's your father".

Needless to say the bar would be full of strangers, mostly farmers in town to buy or sell in the markets for the day. As a matter of course the way he greeted people, my Uncle Kevin was often asked did he know the guys father. It might transpire that the guy's father had long since passed away.

When my uncle Kevin struck up a conversation, if he wanted he could keep the company he was in, plying him with drink for the whole day. He would fascinate them by telling them stories of the countries he travelled to as a merchant seaman when he was abroad. Some stories he told would make the hair on the back of your neck stands up. I often likened him to a Priest back home from the missions. He told true stories as he said, about Voodoo being practised in countries that he was in.

The farmers would be fascinated hearing about the spells that were put on misfortunate guys, trying to scratch out a living on a small patch of land. Kevin would tell then that the pishogery that they know about here in Ireland, was nothing compared to what he witnessed abroad.

My uncle was a very likable and knowledgeable person, and could discuss any subject under the sky. He also had great stories to tell of his experiences of travelling around the world, as he spent years as a seaman sailing ships, in the British Merchant Navy during the Second World War years. I know for a fact that he had to abandon ship more than once, and spent hours and sometimes days in the sea waiting to be picked up after the Germans sank his ships.

He had a few market bars that he used to visit on a regular bases, and would be asked to change the barrels over for them when they were busy. He was a great man to make out earning money. He would usually do what ever he was asked, like picking up glasses, or borrowing a barrel from another bar if the Guinness or Beer ran out. He was often called on to change a barrel if they were busy in the bars. He also knew how to deal with a troublesome customer if he needed to be restrained.

He was always on hand and was a regular sight in the early morning market bars. His nickname in the early part of his life was Tosh but in the latter part of his life everyone knew him, as how's your father. He once told me as a young lad of about twelve he used to help the farmers and their wives to carry heavy bags and baskets of stuff that they purchased from Mrs. Hanley's grocery shop in William Street to the Horse Depository in Glentworth Street.

There were several places around the city where farmers stabled their horse and traps, when they came to town to do their shopping at different holiday times in the year. As I already said my Uncle was well able to make out from a very early age. On another occasion he told me he was asked to ride a horse that some farmer had bought at the horse fair. He was instructed to take the horse to the farmers home about ten miles outside the city.

My Uncle built up a reputation from a very early age living in Garryowen and from frequenting the markets, that stood to him after the war and on into his old age. When war broke out he made his way by thumbing up to Northern Ireland to Saint Patrick's Barracks in a place called Ballymena, County Antrim, to join the British Army. The Regiment he joined was the 1st Battalion of the Royal Ulster Rifles they were an infantry regiment.

He signed on for three years and served with them on a number of dangerous campaigns. His regiment were the first British Regiment to cross over the River Rhine into Germany. He told me the whole Battalion flew in on silent glider airplanes at night; many of his mates were killed before they hit the ground. When it was time for him to get de-mobbed. He re-enlisted to join the British Merchant Navy for a bit more adventure, and to see a bit more of the world. It's from his times in the Merchant Navy; his talent for telling fascinating stories came. He always liked the thought of travelling in ships to see different parts of the world.

There were very few ports around the world that the ships he sailed on didn't enter. He never came home without bringing some kind of a souvenir from the places he travelled to. My Uncle died as a result of a fall outside the Moose Bar in Cathedral Place making his way home, after having a few drinks with his friends. He lived for a few weeks before he threw the towel in and called it a day. There isn't a time that I don't think of him and all his mates any time I pass the old haunts in and around the market bars in Limerick City.

If there were only a way to make those old haunts give up the secret conversations that were held inside their walls, it would make a best seller. The memories I carry with me are priceless to me. They make me feel honoured and privileged to have been around, when those people roamed the streets and frequented those pubs that I'm writing about in Limerick. I hope and trust that there is someone somewhere writing down or making notes of what's happening in their local hostelries for future references.

In my time the invention of sending messages by racing pigeons was talked about. It moved on to Morse code, and then to telephones and radio, then moved on to television then to a man walking on the moon, was the big topic of conversation. Now the greatest thing since sliced bread is digital satellite television and mobile phones transmitting moving pictures to one another around the world with the click of a button. It's amazing how far we have come in the world, since I first saw a horse drawn carriage on the streets of Limerick.

My final word on the Moose Bar is it is still in the hands of the Tobin family, they have spent a fortune on renovating it and bringing it up to the twenty first century. They have also acquired two better-known public houses in Limerick City, which I hope to mention in other chapters. These purchases were made as a result of winning a large amount of money on our National Lottery. It's good to know that they are in good hands, and are worthy of a visit.

Chapter 9
The Grand Stand

The Grand Stand public house is a few doors up from the Moose Bar in Cathedral Place. It's facing one of the main gates that would take you into the Haymarket and is practically facing the statue of Patrick Sarsfield on the Church grounds of Saint John's Cathedral. I was taken to this public house at a very young age. I remember this public house it was known as Margaret Maloney's.

P.J. Madden was a nephew of Margaret Moloney and he ran it until it was sold to several owners to the present day it is now called the Sarsfield Bar. There used to be a great crowd going into this bar in Maddens time. Quite a lot of Shell Oil lorry drivers made it their local, and every one of those men in my opinion were the best men I ever saw to drink porter. Maddens bar was divided into two bars the public and the lounge each had it's own entrance. You had access to either bars from two different ways when you were inside.

There was a back room in this pub when old Madden had it and it was strictly for playing and listening to operatic music. Guys could bring in their own selection of records to play them. It was fascinating to watch the real connoisseurs of the opera world, trying to reach the top notes of the singer they were listening to them as they tried to sing along with them. Michael Walsh from Kilalee was one that comes to mind. You couldn't even whisper when the records were playing, but the guy that brought in the record could do what he liked, and so it was with anyone that brought his own record to be played.

In later years the upstairs part of the public house was converted into a separate lounge bar or function room. The place to be on any given day of the week was in the public bar area. There used to be a bar maid by the name of Molly Donnelly filling pints in this bar she was often relieved by a barman his name was Joe Storan. Both of those people were the best I ever saw to fill the perfect pint of Guinness.

You wouldn't want to take your eyes off another bar maid that worked there, her name was May Brodie she was a first cousin of P.J. Madden she lived overhead the public house at one time she never married. She sort of went with the bar when P.J. inherited it. Most of the regular guys kept a close eye on May when she started filling pints.

May was just deadly for doctoring the pints; she didn't believe it throwing slops away at all. My brother Donal used to have war with her over it and often reported it to P.J. Madden or his wife, all to no avail. She had a habit of slipping out to the opposite bar from where you called the drink, then suddenly started topping it up in the bar that you called it in. May was just one of those people that couldn't be told. She was so set in her miserly ways that it got worse as she got older. She thought at sometime in her life that some rich farmer would come into the pub and sweep her off her feet, alas it wasn't written in the great book to be.

Poor May was left on the shelf after devoting most of her life to trying to skimp and save for her employers that didn't give a damn about her in the first place. I like to remember her the way she was, when she first came into Limerick City to work for

Margaret Moloney, and when the pub was full of bachelor farmers. She had a few chances but blew it looking for the right guy. Unfortunately time marches on and the longer she waited the task got harder for poor May. I wouldn't mind but she looked pretty good as a rosy cheeked young farmers daughter, when she first came to live and work in Limerick City.

I have seen many changes have taken place since Maddens Bar changed hands.

Kevin O'Mara a brother of Tony O'Mara of (O'Mara Motors Toyota fame), who I mention in another chapter purchased this public house and installed a manager to run it by the name of Gerry Power. I must say that Gerry Power managed to hold on to all the old customers that frequented the bar when P J Madden ran it.

Some of the old staff stayed on with the new management with the exception of May Moloney. She definitely had no chance of being kept on. I loved drinking in the bar under Gerry Powers management. The one thing he couldn't tolerate was trouble in the public house, and that suited my friends and I down to the ground.

Gerry Power was really a great guy I always liked him. Before he took to managing a public house Gerry used to work for my uncle Tony in Danus Clothing Factory. He was also a great soccer player he played for Fairview Rangers and won an F.A.I. Minor Cup medal with them. He was a local man from the fair green, he also lived long enough to run a public house for himself in William Street, and I hope to mention it in another chapter. I'm sad to say Gerry is no longer with us he died a young man.

Every time I went into or came out of Maddens bar I couldn't help thinking of one of the worst beatings I ever got from a Catholic

Priest when I was a small child. All this happened just across the road from Maddens public house. When the time of year was right for knocking conkers down off the trees. St John's Hospital was the first location we went to, the trees were more accessible in the hospital grounds or outside the boundary wall.

But when all the choice conkers was gone off of those trees, the next place we went for them was Cathedral Place. Between Patrick Sarsfield's monument and the Hay Market where there were huge conker trees growing. All of those trees were in the church grounds. But if you were in the Hay Market, you had a better chance of knocking the conkers off the trees. There was a stonewall running from Cathedral Place up to O'Donovan-Rossa Avenue, otherwise known as Rossa Villas. This wall divided the Parish Priests house and Saint Johns Convent School from the Hay Market.

When you were in the Hay Market you had plenty of room to stand back and see where the conkers were that you wanted to knock down. You took aim and threw a stone or a piece of a timber to dislodge a bunch of conkers from the tree. When all the conkers was knocked down from the Hay Market side, the next place to get them was from Cathedral Place.

There was a long concrete air-raid shelter built in Cathedral Place, this building was about twenty foot long and eight foot high and had a solid wooden door on each end at the footpath side. By climbing on top of this building you had a great vantage point for getting at the conkers.

I remember bigger boys than me climbing on top of that and knocking down the conkers for us. Most of the kids from all over the area would come there for their conkers. I happened to go there one day and I pushed open the iron gate leading into the Priests house to pick up whatever conkers were lying on the ground around the trees.

Suddenly the door opened and one of the Priests ran out, no warning what so ever. I got such a fright that I started to run for the gate.

Before I managed to get to the gate he dived at me with a rugby tackle and knocked me to the ground. He caught me by the hair of my head and dragged me back to the Priests house. Our boy's Convent school was directly behind the Priest house. He never asked me what my name was, or where I lived or who my father or mother was. He was just dead bent on giving me the hiding of my life. I just did not deserve what that Priest did to me that day.

I don't hold grudges but long after that event I often wished that the hand that held the stick that beat me so severely on that day would wither and fall off. I have long since asked God for forgiveness for that thought and offered up what ever pain I suffered as a penance but the effect of that beating will always stay with me for ever unfortunately.

Chapter 10
The Geraldine Bar

The Geraldine Bar was once known as Hodkenson's it is situated on the corner of James Street and lower Gerald Griffin Street. The old Dispensary was on the corner facing the public house, and Crosses funeral undertakers is at the other corner, both premises are alongside one another. Both premises complement one another and serve the people that frequent them. The Geraldine bar is the nearest public house to Crosses funeral parlour, and always gets a spill over from people attending removals at Crosses.

The side door going into the Geraldine bar was very near the narrow road between Crosses funeral home and the public house. I often wondered why a railing wasn't put outside the door to stop guys walking straight out on to the road, especially if they had too much to drink. The volume of traffic using that busy road was unbelievable at times. Cars driving through that short road from lower Gerald Griffin Street to John's Square would drench whoever was walking on the footpath on a rainy day.

There used to be some great old characters drinking in the Geraldine bar that I can remember. Most of them would frequent all the market bars around at the time. Funnily enough the Geraldine bar did not have a market licence to open early in the mornings. I found that rather strange, as the Geraldine bar was very near and was only two streets away from the heart of all the markets. I happened to find out this little bit of information by accident, when I met a cork man that worked for over forty years delivering Beamish stout to the public houses in Limerick City.

Directly behind the Geraldine bar was a timber yard it was owned by Dave Dundon. In the wintertime he often had his men cut trees up for firewood and sold them to the general public. I was often sent to get a bag of blocks for the fire as a young lad growing up in Garryowen. The man on the electric saw didn't mind me looking at him. He would be pointing stakes so that they could be easily driven into the ground when the farmers bought them for fencing posts.

Another yard that had men cutting timber that I can remember was over in Cathedral Place. I was very inquisitive as a little boy and always followed the noise of machinery cutting timber. Sometimes I would be hunted away but more often than not I would be left look at what was going on. The noise would be coming from Molloy's builders yard; I used to watch the carpenters working in the workshop at the back end of the yard. They would be making windows and doors getting ready for when the building started up again around the month of March.

Molloy's employed a lot of men working on building sites all around Limerick. They built houses and roads and footpaths. During the Second World War they built air raid shelters in different parts of the city. I used to stand on one of them knocking conkers off the trees, especially the one that was built beside the road at the Sarsfield monument in Cathedral Place when I was a young lad. They were made of solid reinforced concrete about eight foot wide and twenty foot long and about eight foot high.

Guys that would be taken short after leaving the pubs used them as toilets. They were pitch dark inside and the smell out of them was unbearable. I once remember going into one of them and lighting a newspaper, all you could see was lines of shit along the bottom of the walls where it was used as a toilet. Those air raid shelters had a wooden door at either end that was always open. There was no other form of light only the small bit of daylight that was barely visible if you looked from end to end.

The best days work the powers to be ever did was to knock those filthy things down. I remember one of my uncles working for Molloy's in the demolition of the one in Cathedral Place. In those days they used sledge and jackhammers to break up the concrete. With the amount of reinforcing steel bars they had their work cut out to demolish them. There was another builders yard owned by the Early's on the corner of Brennan's Row at the Cathedral end and behind Hanley's house in Cantors Range. I often visited the workshop looking at the carpenters working making doors and windows.

To get back to the Geraldine bar there was a carpenter by the name of Jack McGrath drinking in the Geraldine bar who had just come out of Molloy's yard after looking for a job. The story he told was priceless to listen to him it went something like this. Jack called to the office in Molloy's yard and asked the young lad that was behind the counter if he could see Mr Molloy. The young lad went into the back office and told Mr Molloy there was a man waiting to see him.

"Mr Molloy told the lad to ask the man what he wanted as he was too busy, to see him". The young lad asked the man, "What he wanted as Mr. Molloy was too busy to see him". "Jack sent the young lad back into the boss to say he was a carpenter, and that he was looking for a job". The boy delivered the message and was sent back to tell the man, "That Mr. Molloy said to come back in the spring". "Jack told the young lad to go back into Mr. Malloy and tell him that he was a carpenter not a cuckoo".

The Geraldine bar always done good business out of the huge crowds visiting Crosses Funeral Parlour to attend funerals. I had many a drink in that public house after seeing a member of my own family or friends of mine being laid out in Crosses funeral home. The Crosses were in the business of undertaking since before the famine in 1847. Joe Cross once showed me the family books that dated back to 1845. My recollection of seeing the beautiful raised engraved glass panelled horse drawn hearse still is clearly visible in my memory. Likewise the highly groomed jet-black carriage horses, pulling the immaculately highly polished black carriages.

To my knowledge Crosses employed all local labour to groom and look after the many horses stabled in the huge yard that they owned between Gerald Griffin Street and Brennan's Row. When they dressed up the horses in their highly polished black leather harness and polished the horse's hoofs with a mixture of black engine oil. It was their turn to dickey themselves up in three-quarter length black kaki-like coats with rows of gleaming silver buttons. They wore tall hard hats with black hackles on them to top it off.

Two men dressed in similar garb drove the four white horses pulling the hearse. The control those drivers had over those horses was an amazing sight to see. The custom in those days was to throw the soapy water including the soap that was used to wash and shave a corpse, after the hearse before it left the house. I witnessed that practice many times as a young lad growing up in Garryowen.

I'm glad to say the Geraldine Public house and Crosses funeral undertakers are still with us to day. Both establishments are up to date with Crosses using state of the art motor vehicles and plush rooms for visitors paying their respect to their dead. While the Geraldine bar has come on in leaps and bounds, and is a great place for finger licking grub while listening to good music, or watching a football match on television.

I had the pleasure of visiting this public house with my good friend Jimmy Mulcahy a few days after Christmas, and wanted to visit it before the year 2002 was over. I was pleasantly surprised to see many of my old friends enjoying drinking good-looking pints of creamy headed pints of Guinness. All in jolly mood and judging from some of my old mates like Richard (Dickey) Keane and his dear wife and twin sister and her husband, sitting in the bar. I knew the singsong wasn't far off. Dickey Keane is a very good friend of mine and well able to render a verse of a beautiful song.

He also played soccer with my brother Donal for Geraldine's. In his day he was someone to be reckoned with, when he played soccer one would think he had a soccer ball glued to the toe of his boot. For the world he used to remind me of one of the all time English greats called Stanley Mathews. Unfortunately I was unable to stay in this very promising company of potential singers, as I had to take off urgently. The barman called a taxi and within minutes I was whizzing my way home from the Geraldine Bar to my home in the upper part of town.

That visit done me the world of good and I promised myself to make a return visit and hopefully meet and hear a few of the old songs, bringing more memories back to me of the old bars that are still to be found in Limerick City.

Chapter 11

The Square Bar

The Gaelic Bar as it was known then, is situated on the corner of John Square, and is facing the fountain in St Johns Square; it is one of the corner houses in the small range of houses known as Cantor's Range. In the early forties in was owned by a man I just barely remember as Tommy Curtin. Tommy Curtin sold it to Jim Noonan and he sold it to Joe Barry, who married a niece of Jim Noonan's called Mary Kirby, they now own it. If you like it is still in the same family as it has been for well over fifty years.

Of all these early morning pubs the one my grand father favoured most was the Gaelic Bar, it's now called the Square Bar, and all the public houses that I ever drank in from about 1970 to 1980 the square bar took the biscuit for good company and enjoying the singsong and having the crack. The fact that my only brother Donal, and a lot of my schoolmates, and all of my friends and neighbours from Garryowen, and the surrounding areas frequented this glue pot, may have had a lot to do with it.

Many times I remember sitting on my fathers lap in this pub, and hearing him say after he blew the froth off his pint, to let my little nose into his glass to drink the black stuff. "Drink it up son it will kill the worms in your belly".

Strangely when I started to write about this pub my nephew Michael O'Donovan my brother's son, sent me an e/mail from America saying he remembered his father saying the very same thing to him. Is it any wonder they call the public houses in Ireland Chemist shops?

All the Markets opened around five o'clock in the morning, and the public toilets had to be open when the Farmers came into town. My grandfather used to leave the house every morning around 4 30am he would finish at 1 pm. He always went for a drink to the Square Bar in St John's Square after finishing work.

The kind of stuff you would be exposed to on any given day or night went something like this. I was listening to my grandfather telling a story one day, about when he used to open the public lavatory in Upper William St. on the early morning market days when he was working for the Limerick Corporation.

He went on to say he was sitting having a drink one freezing cold winter's day and some smart guy, was trying to take the piss out of him. The smart Guy asked my grandfather was it cold when he got up for work that morning, when everyone else was in bed.

My grandfather looked at him as only he could to size the guy up, and after thinking about it for a while he started preparing his pipe for a smoke he then said. "I was passing down Cathedral Place this morning and would you believe me, it was so cold that no other than the General himself, Patrick Sarsfield, asked me to hold his sword until he clapped his hands". Everyone in the public house burst out laughing, and the smart Guy didn't know where to look. That stopped your man asking stupid questions my grand father said.

It's listening to stuff like that that kept me going back to the same pubs where all those old characters used to hang out. Can you just imagine listening to two old guys talking about calling one another in the morning for work? One fellow says to the other, "If I have left before you call to my house in the morning I will leave a newspaper sticking out of the letter-box. That will be the signal for you not to knock". "Ok the other fellow said and if I get there before you leave for work I will take it out."

The amount of men I had the pleasures of spending time with over a drinking session, most of them I knew personally but who are no longer with us. But when I think of them I can't help but laugh at the funny sayings and the jokes they told. I remember one time there was a pub quiz on in the square bar. The quizmaster asked one of the square bar team, "What is the correct name to describe a baby Bear". Your man thought for a few seconds then blurted out, "A Teddy bear". He brought down the house with laughter. Needless to say the guy nearly died with embarrassment.

He felt a little better later on, when one of the opposing team from the Pike Bar, a character called, Toddy Short, another comedian in his own right. Toddy got his nickname not because he was a small guy but because he was tall. Toddy was asked to " Spell Paint". Toddy's face reddened up and answered, "What colour". That answer brought the house down also. Some of the characters that took part in some of those pub quizzes would have you in stitches laughing for days after.

The square bar as I already said was like a glue pot when you went in it was very hard to leave it the crack was so good. I can honestly say I never had a dull moment drinking in that bar with my friends. I often felt at times after spending the best part of the day in there, that I was actually drinking myself sober. The only time we would leave it was for a change of scenery.

I was in there another time and this guy asked me, if I had heard the one about the two mind readers that bumped into one another in the street. I said "no", he said, "One fellow said to the other your fine; how am I?"

I remember one day I was in there and there were two clients drinking standing at the bar counter. Both of them were steamed up to the gills and getting ready for the road to go home. Suddenly the door into the bar opened and this stranger came in and asked to use the toilet. The bar man said, "Over there pointing to the toilet door".

The stranger called for a small power whiskey, and then proceeded to go in to the toilet. The two-boozed guys at the bar were oblivious to what was going on around them. The barman filled the small power whiskey and left it on the counter. He turned away for a few seconds to answer the phone. One of the drunks at the bar picked up the small power whiskey and demolished it with one swig. Poor man came out of the toilet and was standing at the counter waiting for the barman to serve him.

The barman turned round and said to your man, "That will be one pound fifty please". Your man looked surprised and said to the bar man, "But you never gave it to me". The barman showed your man the empty glass and said to him, you must have drank it before you went into the toilet. Poor man looked puzzled scratched his head he then paid the barman and walked out the door. I later pointed out what happened to the barman. That was one potential customer I'm sure that the square bar lost for good.

There was a mixture of characters using the Square Bar in those days. One guy I remember my brother Donal gave him the nickname, "Stand bye for lumps". The reason being he used to stand at the end of the counter beside the front door leading into the bar, and it was practically impossible to come in or go out of the bar without bumping into him. No matter how many guys that bumped into him he just wouldn't move away to keep the entrance clear.

The barman often put his drink middle ways up the counter to get him to move back from the door, no good he wound up back in the same place. He never sat down just stood in the same place. Fortunately he wasn't a guy that could drink a session of porter, three pints was about his limit, but it took him one and a half hours to finish them. Needless to say no one liked to see this guy in the bar, especially if there was a couple of funerals on. I often heard it said in the toilet, "Thanks be to Jesus stand bye for lumps is gone out of the pub".

The space inside the square bar was fairly tidy. The seating started behind the front door at the right hand side as you entered the bar. It ran all around the square room and finished at the toilet door at the other end of the bar counter. The barrels were conveniently stored under the open fronted seating. No matter where you happened to be sitting you had a perfect view of everyone standing or seated in the bar. It was the ideal cosy place to meet friends to have a singsong or tell jokes.

Every now and again some comedian or other would appear and start telling jokes. Quite a lot of tradesmen frequented the square bar. I remember on one occasion a carpenter was telling a story about a guy that worked on the same building site as him. The carpenter was cutting roof rafters and observing the poor man climbing up the ladder. He had difficulty climbing up the ladder and appeared to be struggling as the sole of his boot was hanging off and catching on the rungs of the ladder.

Suddenly the boss arrived on site and saw what was happening. He called the man down to talk to him, and after a few moments took out what looked like a wad of pound notes. He stripped off something and handed it to the poor man, and walked away. The carpenter asked the man what the boss said to him. He said, "The boss told him he might be able to help him, and took out a wad of money; he gave him the rubber band and told him to put it on his shoe". Poor man thought he was going to get the price of a new pair of boots. Listening to that story brought the house down with laughter.

Many changes have taken place around the market bars and surrounding areas from when I first knew them; most of them were for the better, others I'm not so sure. I don't mind making changes by enlarging the premises to accommodate more seating. But when the whole atmosphere of the public house is changed, I personally would have preferred if the yuppie architects, consulted with some of the old patrons that now frequent the premises they designed.

On a recent visit to the Square bar I was very impressed to see the amount of space that they gained by knocking the two houses that were beside it, and converting it into one large establishment. I couldn't find fault with the outside appearance of the place. But as I entered the feeling that came over me was rather strange. Gone was the great feeling I used to have on entering the old establishment I knew so well.

As I sat in two different parts of this now modern bar observing the views of the two squares outside, I tried to get the old feeling I always got when I used to drink in this bar. Being in the presence of some of my old friends like Jimmy Mulcahy, Stephen Hayes, and Gerry McMahon helped, as we sat recalling the great times and laughter we had on this same spot of ground before the new renovation job was done.

I got the feeling that the old guys that are no longer with us, like Sean and Stephen Healy, two brothers, that would make you laugh just to see them come into the bar. You knew you were in for a treat when they came in. The old timers like Ger Madden and Christy, (The Devil) Hayes, the McManus brothers all pork butchers. I just couldn't feel their presence, to me it's as if their spirits left when the walls were knocked down of the old public house that I loved so well. I couldn't help but agree with them.

The modern architects of today seem to be catering for the yuppie visitors of tomorrow, rather than our own generation of young and older citizen's. Even Saint John's Cathedral is getting a new facelift. My friends and I decided to look for a pub, where the atmosphere was more familiar to us. Especially around Christmas time when we tried to re-live the great old memories of our friends, who are no longer with us.

Chapter 12
The Holy Ground

The Holy Ground Bar is situated on one corner of Saint Johns graveyard in the Johns Square area of Limerick. It is numbered as 1, Church Street, and is the only public house that I know of that is actually built in a graveyard. I frequented this establishment on many occasions and have seen it change hands many times. It's about the smallest public house I was ever in, in my life. When the upstairs part was converted into a lounge bar. When this job was done it was a great place to take your girlfriend or wife to listen to a good sing song.

I remember drinking up there and listening to some of the best singers I ever had the pleasure of hearing. The only trouble was trying to negotiate the narrow stairs on the way down, and the men's toilet was on the ground floor. The first time I went into this public house to do some serious drinking, was with my brother Donal in the Month of June 1967.

I know this because I was only after coming home from London with two of my sons Michael and Noel. We had joined in the Corpus Christy procession from outside Saint Josephs Church in O'Connell Avenue, and walked down to Saint John's Cathedral, to attend the open air Mass. I got the fright of my life that same day as my two little sons ran away from me and I couldn't find them in the huge crowds of people marching and spectators looking on at both sides of the road all the way down to Saint John's Square.

I eventually found them around the Mass alter built outside the Cathedral. Bare in mind those two little boys were born in London and it was their first time ever in Limerick City. I could hardly understand their accent not to mind a stranger, so I was very grateful for getting them back safely. I met my brother in the crowd and we decided to go to the Holy Ground bar for a drink, God knows I needed that to settle my nerves.

The reason I was home from England was I had a daughter killed outside our house in London on the 28th of April 1967. My little son Noel saw it happen and as a result used to wake up at night having nightmares. My wife thought it would be good if I brought him to Ireland with one of his brothers to get his mind off of it for a while. It would do me good as well for I couldn't stop crying thinking about it.

My brother Donal pointed to a man sitting at the bar, and told me a story about a man that came from Garryowen, who had been a lorry driver and his job entailed delivering coal. Twelve Months before hand he had a son that was killed by a lorry crossing over the road. He had a hard time trying to get over that. Only to be driving in Clare Street one day and children were skipping with a rope on the road as they often did.

The kids left the rope down to let the lorry pass over, and just as it was passing one child pulled the rope, unfortunately it was tied to the waist of another child at the other side of the road. The rope was caught up on the wheels of the lorry dragging the child in and was killed instantly. I have often heard it said you might think your case is bad until you hear about someone else's. The loss of a young child is bad and something one never gets over.

But to be in that mans shoes after hearing what my brother told me I cried for him, and I had a fairly good idea of what he was going through. I still mourn the loss of the only daughter I ever had her name was Caroline, and she would be thirty-six if she were alive today. One good way of getting over the loss of someone you loved is to be in good company in a snug little public house, the Holy Ground bar fills that bill.

One great character that frequented this establishment and is no longer with us was married to my mother's sister Kathleen Donovan. His name was Christy Mulqueen he originally came from Castle Connell Co, Limerick. He was the best man I ever heard to recite recitations. Some of those verses would go on for ages sometimes twenty or thirty at a time. But it was the way he could pull it off without boring the person listening to them. He might start off with the charge of the Light Brigade.

"Half a league, half a league onward.
All in the valley of death rode the six hundred.
Forward the light brigade, charge for the guns, he said,
To the valley of death rode the six hundred.
Forward the light brigade was there a man dismayed
Not though the soldier knew, someone had blundered,
Theirs not to make reply, theirs not the reason why,
Theirs but to do and die, into the valley of death,
Rode the six hundred.
Cannon to right of them, cannon to left of them,
Cannon in front of them, volleyed and thundered,
Stormed at, with shot and shell, holed the road and well.
Into the jaws of death, into the mouth of hell,
Rode the six hundred.

Flashed as they turned in the air, sabering and gunners their,
Charging an army while, all the world wondered,
Plunged in the battery smoke, right through the line they broke,
Cossack and Russian weald, from the sabres stroke,
Shattered and sundered, then they rode back,
but not the six hundred.
Cannon to right of them, cannon to left of them,
Cannon behind them, volleyed and thundered,
Stormed in which shot and shell, while horse and hero fell,
They that had fought so well, came through the jaws of death,
Back from the mouth of hell, all that was left of them,
left of six hundred.
When can their glory fade, oh! the wild charge they made,
All the world wondered, honoured the charge they made,
Honoured the light brigade, noble six hundred".

Christy Mulqueen was an uncle of the famous ballad singer Ann Mulqueen; she lives in Ring County Waterford and is a publican's wife. Ann Mulqueen is a regular ballad singer on Radio Eireann programs. All Christy Mulgueen's daughters are very talented singers. This talent has broken out in Christy Mulgueen's grandchildren the Gardiner's and the Coleman's to name but two families, and they can be heard singing in quite a few public houses to the present day in Limerick City.

The local drinkers from around the locality that frequented the Holy Ground bar, I always found very interesting to talk to. They were the kind of guys that would answer you with a question. For instance if you asked any one of them would they like to have a drink? They might say to you, "Can a duck swim", or say "Do you really want to know"? Or " Are you buying". The Yank jokes always gave our American friends a laugh.

One particular friend of mine whose name is Paddy Hanley and who originally hails from Cantors Range just around the corner in St Johns Square. One of his favourite jokes that he often told about the American Bald Eagle went something like this.

He would ask his captive American audience, "What the wingspan of the American Bald Eagle was, when he flew away from the sun?" Naturally the answer might be four feet from wing tip to wing tip. Paddy would then switch the question and ask them, "What was it when he flew straight into the sun"? Of course the Yanks would say, "The same". No Paddy would say shading his eyes by closing one of his arms from the elbow, and cupping his hand shading his eyes and going through the motion of flying with one wing. He would then say, "Don't forget the eagle is bald".

I never had a dull moment in that public house as often as I frequented it.

On the opposite corner of the Holy Ground pub is one of the most famous fish and chip shops in Limerick City, and I'm pleased to say they are still feeding the people of Garryowen and surrounding areas to this present day. As far back as I can remember it was always called Donkey Fords chip shop. It's still in business by the same family only two or three generations, on from old Mister ford that I knew as a child growing up in Garryowen.

You would be drawn to that fish and chip shop from miles around, by that gorgeous smell that couldn't help to find your nostrils as you walked the Irish Town. Every Friday Donkey Fords fish and chips were eaten for dinner in every house in the locality. The gift of having a drink in the Holy Ground Bar was you could nip over the road, tap on the hatch at the side window of the chipper, and ask one of the Fords to wrap up a take away telling them where you were.

When the grub was ready they would bring it over to the pub to you. Many were the take a way's that was eaten in the pub before taking them home as it was intended to do in the first place. Usually when the smell of the fish and chips came into the pub, it set off a rush for the chipper. The temptation was too great to resist, another great advantage after eating a feed from Donkey Fords chipper was you would feel like drinking Lough Erin after it.

The tricks that I remember guys getting up to in that chipper when I was a young lad growing up in Garryowen. The salt that you would use in that chip shop used to be kept in small tins that used to contain Andrews liver salts at one time. When they were filled up with salt, a few holes were punched in the lid before it was tightly sealed for people to use to salt their fish and chips.

The vinegar bottles were just lemonade bottles with their tops perforated with holes to let the vinegar sprinkle out. It was fun to see a drunken man drench his fish and chips with vinegar only to see him put the salt as he thought over the lot and see it fizzing up in front of him. Little did he know that someone was after putting Andrews liver salt into the tin that held the salt?

I used to see Mr Ford coming in his donkey and cart to the chip shop with bucket loads of freshly cut chips ready to be fried. It seemed a never-ending job to keep the chips coming, to my knowledge they were always cut by hand in the family home just off of John Street. I was fascinated to see a contraption fixed to a table in the chip shop that done away with the entire cutting chips by hand.

The new way cut a whole potato with one pull of a handle, the spud was placed over a plunger when it was pulled down it pushed the spud through a sharp grid and the chips fell into a bucket under the table. Doing it this way if you placed the spud the long way up the chips were longer when they were cut. So much for the Holy Ground public house and Donkey Fords chip shop, they are a great combination and should never be separated from one another.

Chapter 13
The Launch Bar

The Launch Bar as it is now called is situated in John Street otherwise known as the Irish Town. I knew it as The Punch Bowel, it's a couple of doors down from Donkey Fords chip shop, and is also one of the early morning market bars. There was an old mattress factory between the public house and Donkey Fords chip shop; this was a stone building three floors high. I remember a pulley wheel being used to lift bales of material up to the top floor of this building; likewise the same system was used to lower stuff down to the ground.

There was a stone inserted into the wall of this building marking something bad that had happened back in the penal times in Ireland. From the stories I heard as a child but never really confirmed. It seems that a woman was hanged from this building for defying some law or other back in the seventeenth century. The stone makes some reference to the woman as the brazen head. This stone was removed sometime in the early nineteen seventies. It can be seen today set in the sidewall of some steps leading up to 101, O'Connell Street and right beside a public house they call the Brazen Head in 102, O'Connell Street in Limerick City. The inscription on the stone reads,

"The old Brazen Head built by Simon Kent 1794". It should have never been taken from its original place in that building in the Irish Town.

My first memories of the bar known as the Punch Bowl, was when I went to school in St Johns Christian Brothers School, a couple of doors down from the pub. I had occasion to look in to it on my way home from school in the late forties, I remember they used to have the old town gas lights on in it. My memories of the school were something else.

When I went to Saint John's Christian Brother's school, down in the Irish Town. There were four Christian brothers teaching in that school when I went there. The worst child beater of all was Br. Broderick in my opinion he showed no mercy at all and second to him was Br. Murray, he wasn't half as bad. Out of the four, two were good charitable understanding schoolteachers. The other two were just pure sadistic trash. All they wanted to do was beat children; beat them; day in and day out for no apparent reason at all.

I spent nearly three years in that school and I suppose I spent the rest of my life trying to forget those years. For what I saw then I still remember to this present day. The things I saw dished out to other children and sometimes to myself was pure unadulterated cruelty, to pure innocent children. I saw young fellows coming into school on a freezing cold winter's morning; some of them may not have had a cup of hot water in their stomachs or a slice of bread. They were so terrified of being beaten with a cane or leather strap, after sleeping it out and being late for school.

I saw boys coming into school in their bare feet; sometimes their toes were bleeding, maybe after stubbing their toes on the ground running into school. I saw them being called up to the top of the classroom. They were told to hold out their freezing cold hands to be slapped for being late for school. I used to cringe with fear first and then pity, for those defenceless classmates of mine that were called up, to be punished with a cane or leather strap. Boys came from all over Limerick to go to that school. I made friends with guys that came in all the way from as far away as Thomond Gate and Saint Munchin's Parish and the Island field and places like that.

To make you're way into school from those areas on a cold winters day especially if it was raining. You would be drenched to the skin and you had no way of drying yourself out. Even on the coldest winter mornings I don't ever remember a fire to be lighting in any of the classrooms in that school. To have to face into a big cold classroom with bare floorboards, and the floorboards were so badly worn that the nails were actually sticking up out of the floor.

This was due to constant scrubbing of the timber floors. The nails kept protruding up and were very sharp. To stand on one of those nails especially if a guy wasn't wearing shoes or boots, they were so sharp that you were sure to cut the sole of your foot. Many boys tripped over and stubbed their toes on those nails.

One thing I used to dread seeing was the classroom door opening after the roll call and the prayers were said. To look and see a boy drenched to the skin and maybe shivering with the cold, trying to give some excuse to the Christian Brother for being late for school. No matter what kind of excuse was given, the result was always the same and he was still punished. The next hour for that boy was spent trying to ease the pain and throbbing out of his fingers after getting slapped on both hands. God forgive them but they were cruel sadistic bastards.

I often wondered what kind of homes those men came out of, because there was certainly no love in them, they were just cruel people and that's for sure. How is it possible for a school that has only four classrooms and four Christian brothers teaching one class each, to have half of them child beaters? The big joke is they called themselves Christian brothers. John St. Police Station was next door to the school. All this physical abuse was going on right beside them.

I'm sure if they knew what was going on, they would have taken some of these fellows in and put them behind bars, where they deserved to be for the cruelty they dished out to defenceless children. I would have loved to seen them getting some of their own medicine. Another thing, I never saw a cruelty officer or a Doctor come into our school and check up on us, to see how we were getting on. It is as if the Christian brother's were a law unto their own, and no one would question their methods of teaching or go against them in any way at all.

I got to know the Punch Bowl public house to drink in when I came home from London to live, in August 1970. I had a few carpenter friends that I used to work with in those days, who frequented this early morning drinking establishment. My first impression of this public house at the time was it was a glue pot. Because the guys that used to assemble in it were so interesting, it was practically impossible to leave their company. The slightest shower of rain was enough of an excuse not to go to work for the guys working on building sites. In those days tradesmen had what they called wet time cards. That meant a stamp was put on your wet time card for every week you worked.

If the weather got bad and you were sent into the site hut you had to stay there for two hours to see if the weather would improve. If not then you were paid six hours for that day out of your wet time card. It was a kind of insurance against being rained off. When I worked for the Lanigan Brothers Builders, they built four factories in the dock on the reclaimed old Corcanree city dumpsite.

To get to where the job was from my house I used to cycle down to the Limerick Docks, on a wet and rainy day a decision had to be made. I would be tossing it up on my mind weather to turn left to go to the mucky building site or right to go to the Punch Bowl public house. The weather decided it for me every time, if it was to be the pub, the first thing that had to be done was to get into the job to clock on. When that was done I would slip out through the fence where I had left my bicycle, and race as fast as I could in the dock road to the Punch Bowl public house.

It's amazing the amount of tradesmen that congregated in the early morning public houses. Anyone looking for a tradesman urgently would make their way to the Punch Bowl as one pub among many, to find whatever trade they needed to do a job of work for them. Carpenters, plumbers, electricians, bricklayers, plasterers, labourers, they were all to be found their, and would jump to do a Tom-job as they were called, for a few extra quid in their pocket.

The man that owned the pub in those days was called McGovern he was an ex-policeman. He also took a hand in organizing and training the young boys of Saint Johns boxing club, along with one of our own local men namely John Lee, who was in my class in Saint Johns infant boys school in Garryowen, at the back of Saint Johns Cathedral. Saint Johns boxing club was one of many good boxing clubs in Limerick city; it also had a very good reputation for producing good boxers.

My own son Christopher was a member of the Saint Johns club boxing team, and I remember him travelling as far away as Belfast to compete with other boxing clubs in competitions. John Lee the trainer once told me Christopher had the potential to be a very good boxer. One of the best boxing clubs in Limerick at the time was Saint Francis boxing club. They won loads of trophy's they had a hall in a small lane at the back of Patrick Street and Arthur's Quay, the entrance was from Francis Street the lane was a cul-de-sac.

To my knowledge most guys that wanted to take up boxing at the time would have tried to sign up with Saint Francis boxing club, every other club after that was second choice. Saint Munchin's had a great reputation for turning out good boxers too. Limerick had a good few boxing clubs in different areas of the city; all of them would be trying to get on the Irish team to represent their country.

I remember John Lee telling me his hardest job was going around to public houses trying to collect a few bob to try and keep the boxing gloves and whatever gear they needed up to date. They all wanted to have a boxing club to be proud of but no one wanted to support it financially. Its amazing the kind of memories that keeps flooding back to me, when I think of a place like a public house I frequented at one time or another. So much for the Launch as it is now called.

Chapter 14
Frawley's Bar

Frawley's Bar is situated in Broad Street and is at the junction of Mungret Lane as you leave or enter Broad Street. To my knowledge the present owners of Frawley's public house go back three generations. I must confess I have only visited this well-established public house a few times in my life. What I do know about it is what I have been informed by my son Desmond who frequents it quite often.

From what I remember about it, it was always a very cosy family bar to have a drink in. Most of the regular clientele frequenting this bar would live locally, apart from a few blow inns' that travelled out of Garryowen and Kilalee, to sample other neighbouring pubs hospitality. Back in the early seventies my wife and I used to be on the lookout for good singing public houses. A weekend in Frawley's was one of those cosy bars to visit.

Unfortunately in this day and age Televisions screens put a stop to all that. The usual everyday soaps that swamp our televisions are the order of the day now. No talk or sing song anymore, if it isn't Fair City or Coronation Street or some other distraction like a soccer match or night racing.

Before I forget it there is one guy that I must give a mention to and who has been a good customer of Frawley's over many years. He is an old friend and playmate of mine going back over sixty years. He is none other than the famous photographer Freddie Kenny. Many are the times Freddie snapped my wife and I in one of the ballrooms of romance in Limerick City that was many moons ago I might add.

I remember a maze of lanes on either side of Frawley's public house that would take you into Water Gate. The narrowest of those lanes was right beside Frawley's public house. I often ran in and out of all those lanes playing cowboys as a child, especially after making my way home from the Tivoli cinema after seeing Errol Flynn in one of his cowboy films.

Frawley's public house was facing Patie Browns Pawn Office. Patie Brown's Pawn Office was one of the best-known establishments in Limerick City when I was a child growing up in Garryowen during the Second World War years. There were many stories told about things that happened at different times in public houses in those days, like one I heard from a guy about Frawley's public house. He went on to say a newsvendor pushed open the door on a freezing cold night selling the penny Leader. Mr. Frawley usually had his radio on for the news after the Angelus every night at six o'clock.

The newspaper boy selling the penny Limerick Leader kept the door open. This didn't help his case one little bit, the misfortunate little boy had a slight impediment also, and was struggling to get the words Limerick Leader out. Mr. Frawley told him close the door and go away, and said, "We get all our news on the radio". The newspaper boy looked at him and said, "That, that's all right Mr Frawley, but, but, but you can't wipe your arse with the radio". Little did Mr Frawley think at the time that, that story would be talked about for years in pubs in Limerick.

Across the road from Frawley's public house was one of the most famous Pawnshops in Limerick City. Patie Browns Pawn office was known all over Limerick city. Many was the wedding ring or pair of shoes or suits pawned to keep some families alive in the hard times during the Second World War years in Limerick City. Patie Brown lived in Cathedral Villas, on the Garryowen Road.

I suppose there wasn't a family living in Limerick in those days that didn't use Patie Browns Pawn Office, to hock something to get money in desperate times to put food on the table. There were many pawn shops in Limerick that I can remember but Patie Browns was definitely the one that done the most trade. Crowds of people would be queuing outside on the footpath after getting paid their wages on Fridays and Saturdays all redeeming whatever they pawned earlier in the week.

Patie Brown was looked on as the lifesaver in many houses mid week when the money ran out. The same parcels would be in the Pawn on Tuesday or Wednesday and redeemed a day or so later. Patie couldn't loose and of course the interest may not have been much to start with, but everyone was happy with that set up.

Back in the middle forties where Frawley's was situated it couldn't help but do a roaring trade. I remember Mungret Lane a hive of industry, every shop on both sides of the road had some business or other going on, and they all attracted visitors to the area. There were several eating-houses in the area all doing a roaring trade, the publicans included.

In the days when it was a common sight to see dogs unleashed in public houses with their owners after returning from a long walk up the Plassey bank. I heard one about a stranger that walked into the bar one day, and saw a Jack Russell dog lying on the floor, he must have been an Englishman and a dog lover. The story goes when he went to the bar counter and called for a drink, he asked the owner." Does your dog bite"? "No was the reply he got". The stranger turned and went to pat the Jack Russell on the head, only to be nipped on the fingers with very sharp teeth. He then said to the owner, "I thought you said your dog doesn't bite". "I did, said the owner my dog doesn't bite, the dog that bit you isn't my dog".

Up to a few Months ago I was pleased to see the stalls setting up again in the main street of Mungret Lane. It brought memories of the old days back to me, alas our Fire Chief put a stop to that practice, because I'm told a fire tender couldn't get into the street in case of a fire breaking out, in many of the modern built up flats in the area, how times have changed what a pity?

Chapter 15
Costelloe's Bar

Costello's bar is situated at the right hand corner of the bottom of the Irish Town in Broad St. and was beside the Abbey Bridge. I used to visit this public house with my father when Mick Quilligan owned it. It was a well-established public house and to my knowledge only catered for men. I knew quite a few of Mick's customers, as they happened to be uncles and cousins of mine. All my fathers family both boys and girls used to visit the family home every Sunday to meet. They never failed to meet and find out how each family were making out during the week. If anyone needed help they all mucked in, that was the way things were as I remembered it.

My father and my uncles would decide where they would go for a drink, while my aunties stayed in the house chatting and eating current cake and drinking tea. My uncles would decide whether to visit Willie Curtins Bar in Georges Quay, or Mick Quilligans bar, nine times out of ten Quilligans was the choice, because of the high ceiling as they all smoked.

My cousins and I loved going to Quilligans because it was straight across from O'Sullivan's and Peppers shop. Both of those shops sold the most beautiful ice cream I ever tasted. My dad or uncles never failed to give me the price of ice cream every time they went to the pub.

The first thing that you would notice about the big spacious bar was the huge high wainscoted ceiling. There was a cast iron enclosed round fire grate in the centre of the wooden floor. The heat that radiated out from this little range heated the whole bar. On the coldest night I never heard of anyone complaining in the bar about the cold.

Inside the counter fixed to the back high wall above the optics and mirrors, were square and oval shaped glass cases of several sizes. These housed stuffed wild life in replicas of their own habitat. There were Salmon, Otters, and Wildfowl which done credit to whatever taxidermist's that was responsible for the work that was done on those animals. Those display cases never failed to start up a conversation with newcomers to Mick Quilligans bar.

The first time I ever I had occasion to go in for a drink with my father. Mick Quilligan told me a story about the time he went to school with my father. I remember when my father introduced me to Mick. He told me he was born in 1909 the same year as my father; they grew up and were in the same class in Creagh Lane School in the Parish.

He told me when he made his first Holy Communion he called to my grandmother's house in the Sand Mall. She gave him sixpence that would have been a lot of money in those days bearing in mind my grandmother died in 1924.

The tale Mick told us was about one guy that used to come into his pub; this guy had a reputation for nicking pints when his patrons visited the toilet. Mick decided to teach this fellow a lesson, so he arranged for an old man to sit at the table with a pint in front of him, gamming on to be asleep. The pint that Mick filled was taken from the slop bucket behind the bar.

Low and behold the pint snatcher showed up and sat down beside the old man and was just about to take the old mans pint. The old man woke up by the way, and said to your man, "Would you like to drink that pint". The guy thought all his birthdays were coming together and said, "I will of course". He picked it up and drank it in one swallow". "Jesus said the old man you must have a great constitution, I drank that pint three times and I couldn't keep it down". Mick said he never saw that guy in his public house again. There were quite a lot of sayings going around about fellows that used to nick pints. I heard it said that one patron left a note beside his drink saying, he had put his false teeth into his pint. When he returned from the toilet his pint was gone, and written was another note saying, thanks friend drank your pint couldn't find your false teeth.

Those pint snatchers were a menace to the local public houses in any area where they operated. Unfortunately all the public houses within a radius of a mile or two from Thomond Park were targets for that kind of thing, with thousands of rugby supporters, filling the bars going or coming from rugby matches. Unless you held your drink in your hand all the time, you could never be sure it would be there when you came back from the toilet.

God help any pint snatcher if he was caught by any one of those big strong rugby Shannon supporters. There is no way that sort of thing would be tolerated by any of that crowd. I'd say if any member got their hands on the culprit, he would be thrown in from Mick Quilligans public house, over the Abbey wall into the Abbey River. Having said that I don't want to give the impression that they were violent people. Just good citizens and wouldn't want their part of Limerick to get a bad name, over one or two layabouts who knocked off pints.

There were some lovely singers in the Parish and quite a lot of

them frequented all the local bars, in and outside the boundary of the Parish. Of course the rivalries of songs could be heard all over Limerick City. From the Shannon supporters singing,
" There is an Isle" which is well known as the Parish national anthem. The other side of the coin you might have the Young Munster supporters from the other side of town, up at the back of the Monument. They would be chanting their war cry, "Beautiful, Beautiful Munster".

There was never a dull moment when those two opposing teams and their supporters met on or off the playing fields. I remember one character in particular his nickname was Dollars Mulcahy. He used to dress himself and his dog up, with a cap and jersey in the Young Munster's colours of Black and amber. He also sported a blackthorn stick painted in the same striped colours. They were some sight to see making their way out to Thomond Park Rugby Ground.

If Young Munster won the match it is said Dollars had his dog trained to bark out the winning score. Another one I heard about Dollars and his dog, he was coming back from a funeral one day and, and turned into Jerry O'Deas public house in Mulgrave St. to have a drink. Naturally he had his dog with him, he carried him everywhere he went.

There was a crowd in the bar arguing about how many times Young Munster won the cup in the last ten fifteen years. Of course Dollars was asked to clear up the argument and said the correct amount of times. One guy that didn't agree said to Dollars, "OK, if you're so smart tell me, how many times did Shannon win the Trophy". Dollars looked at his dog then turned to the guy that asked him, and said. " I don't know I haven't the dog that long? Can you just imagine the laughter from all the supporters when they heard that answer?

Rugby was then, and still is, a Sacred Religion between the six rugby teams based in Limerick City to this present day. Is it any wonder that they say Limerick is the home of Rugby? Mick Quilligans public house has long since changed hands and is now owned by John Costello. John is a Kerryman and would follow the Kerry Team to the ends of the earth. He is also a great friend of Paudie O'Shea, the great Kerryfootballer and manager.

I'm delighted to learn that some of my old and dear friends from Sarsfield Avenue Garryowen, are frequenting this old and famous pub that holds such happy memories for me, namely Donal and John O'Connell, Michael Sheehan, Pa McCarthy, Padna Hayes, Willie Keane and Desmond O'Leary when he comes home from the States occasionally, to name but a few the rest are too numerous to name. Final word on this famous old public house, well worth a visit, it's a pity they don't resurrect the old Abbey Regatta. That would really be a treat for visitors to this historic area of the Limerick city I love so well.

Chapter 16
The Locke Bar

The Locke Bar and Restaurant is now under the management of Mrs Jackie Costello and her son Richard. They have acquired quite a few properties and turned them into public houses. The best known of these was formerly an A.I.B. Bank in O'Connell Street in the heart of Limerick city. They acquired another pub called the Bridge Bar in Bishop Street known to me as Rosie Clohessy's Bar.

The Lock Bar is situated in Georges Quay, facing the Abbey River and only a couple of doors down from Bishop Street and Mathew Bridge. When I first knew the Lock Bar it was known as Willie Curtains bar. Willie Curtain was still running his public house and pulling pints of Guinness at over ninety years of age. If he wanted a hand to tap a barrel he could rely on several of his customers to help out in that respect.

Willie Curtain was a retired master carpenter in his day; he worked for Kenny's who were a firm of Limerick Builders. They had a joinery shop facing the Royal Cinema in upper Cecil Street. I remember watching a television programme once in his public house. One of our late Presidents was giving a tour of Aras An Uachtarain in the government buildings in Dublin. This documentary was for the sole purpose of showing off the great workmanship that went into the building of this government building.

Willie Curtain's face lit up when he saw this film, it transpired that he was responsible for some of the great work that was done by him, and the Limerick carpenters and joiners who worked for Kenny's Builders of Limerick in those days. Willie Curtain was always proud of the fact he had one son who was a woodwork teacher in the Technical School in Limerick City. He often said he hoped some of his skills that he thought his son would rub off on some poor youngsters learning their trade from his son Clive.

Willie Curtain lived in the pub with his sister; she was bedridden for years and always stayed up stairs. A nun used to visit her without fail every day to wash and do whatever had to be done. Poor Willie never neglected her and would always check her out from time to time. My father loved to call to Willie Curtain to have a couple of small whiskeys; Willie wouldn't open until late in the afternoon.

My father went to live with his sister Mona to keep her company in 18, Georges Quay, after her husband Bill Moore died. He was retired himself and was delighted to be living back in the Parish again after his second wife died. He used to bring his deck chair across the road and sit under one of the trees beside the Abbey River wall. There were two houses numbered eighteen and nineteen in between Barrington's hospital and Saint Ann's school in Georges Quay, he lived in number eighteen.

I often caught him asleep sitting in the sunshine with his sun hat on and his cigarettes and lighter resting on his newspaper on his lap. He used to be delighted when I called to see him. We often went to Willie Curtains for a drink when I called to see him. If Willie Curtain weren't opened we would go around the corner to Bridge Street to

Johnny and Rosie Clohessy's bar it was called the Bridge Bar. Everything my father needed was very convenient to him and was within easy walking distance from where he lived, if you like it was home from home.

All the guys of his own age he knew since he was a little boy, the school he went to was at the back of Willie Curtains pub and beside Rosie Clohessy's public house, it was called Creagh Lane School. The sub post office was next to the school that is where he used to draw his pension. Above the post office was Broderick's Chemist shop; he collected his medicine there. The other medicines he needed like the odd pint of Guinness or small power whiskey, he got in a huge variety of public houses near by. He loved to meet some of his old school pals and to chat about the things they did as kids. I loved listening to the old boys telling stories about the Black and Tans and how the Irish Republican Army was a constant thorn in their side.

I remember my father telling a story about the time the Black and Tans made a raid on my grandfather's house in 8, Sir Harry's Mall. The whole family were brought out and lined up against the wall. They threatened to shoot his eighteen-year-old brother Dan in front of all the family as being a member of the IRA They relented when my grandmother begged for his life to be saved.

Instead the British Forces herded all the family back into the house and told them to put blankets up to the windows, and told them to lie on the floor away from the windows. They then went across the Abbey River to a public house that was owned by a family by the name of McInerney. They cleared the whole house and blew it to smithereens; my father later told me it was a special meetinghouse for the IRA. Every window for a quarter of a mile around was broken with that blast.

To listen to old Willie Curtain telling stories about the Black and

Tans and how the IRA made fools out of them was something else. The Tans as he used to call them were hated and took their lives into their hands every time they entered any area of the Parish. Snipers would pick them off from many locations where they could make their escape easily. The sewers of Limerick City were a maze of escape routes throughout the City. My Aunties were active members of the IRA they were often used to smuggle guns and ammunition in prams across checkpoints going over the Bridges leading to and from the Parish.

I once asked a man that used to work inspecting the underground drains if it was possible to walk around certain parts of Limerick city, he said "Yes and you could come out in the basements of most tenement houses in the heart of the city". He also told me that, "Active units of the IRA came from every walk of life and they were all familiar with those escape routes in times of emergency. If they could get over the fear of rats and the revolting smell it was useful information to know".

I used to be fascinated by the stories the old boys told over a drink. The stories they told ranged from their time in the Boar war in Africa and the First World War, fighting in France. I remember my grandfather telling a story about when he fought in the Boar War it went something like this. They were always talking about the wars they were in when they fought in the British Army. They seemed to get a great laugh recalling some of the things that happened.

There was a man called Jack Smyth who lived in the Ball Alley in Garryowen he was my grandfather's friend. I remember one night they were talking of how mean Jack was and how they found him out. It happened in the Boer War in Africa. One night they were all sitting around the campfire trying to accumulate enough money to buy some liquor. Everyone was asked in turn if they had any money to contribute to the (kitty or money pool), everyone that had money put in.

Empty bottles were collected and exchanged for drink in the Beer tent; everyone except Jack contributed to the collection. He said he was broke. The drink was bought and the singing started and at the end of the night Jack Smyth was so drunk he had to be carried to his bed. When his trousers, was pulled off of him a load of money fell out on the ground, it was wrapped up in a piece of cloth in his pocket. That's how he was found out and it earned him the nickname "Drunken Jack Smyth the dirty lousy meaner".

Willie Curtain had a great bunch of guys frequenting his public house that came from all over Limerick. They came in from Thomond Gate and Ballananty Beg and seemed to make Willie Curtain's pub their local. On top of that at different times of the year, he may have visitors like bell ringers that came for to ring the bells in competitions from as far away as France or England and choirs came from all over to sing in the old Saint Mary's Cathedral. People that visited Barrington's often called in to buy cigarettes, minerals or drink to take in to patients in hospital. Apart from Mick Quilligans pub further down at Baal's Bridge Willie Curtain's bar was the nearest to the hospital in Georges Quay.

Willie Curtain had a very odd manner at times, I remember being in there at one time with my father. When I went to the counter to buy a small power whiskey, my dad asked me to get another jug of water, he liked to dilute his whiskey with plenty of water. When our drinks came up I handed the jug to Willie to fill it. He looked at it and said sarcastically, "Jesus is all the water gone".

My father attacked immediately saying, "Willie, Jesus once turned water into wine, for Christ sake what's up with you, all I want is a drop of water, give Austin a bucket and he'll get it out of the Abbey

River if it's too much trouble for you to turn on the tap". Poor Willie knew he was after putting his foot in it and turned away scratching his head, "Saying oh dear God save us from rusty nails, knots in timber, and cranky men like Christy O'Donovan Lord save us".

That was an old carpenter's prayer after they hit a nail when sawing timber or a hard knot when driving a nail into it, the other part he just added on to torment my father more. Dad would usually get the final word in by saying to Willie, "If you keep this up you will drive me out of your pub into Rosie Clohessy's around the corner and I won't come back anymore".

With that Willie would say, "Christy I have to go up stairs to see does her "Highness" want a cup of tea or something, and while I'm at it I might as well have one myself, will you keep an eye on the shop, if I'm wanted just give me a shout". With that he started to climb up stairs to tend to his sisters needs. Bear in mind Willie was over ninety years of age himself. I used to say to my father when they made Willie Curtain they broke the mould, meaning his likes will never be seen again. So much for Willie Curtain and the bar he had in Georges Quay.

Chapter 17
The Mall Bar

J.Cowhey's Mall Bar when I knew it was called Angela Conway's bar, it is situated in the Sand Mall; it's only a short walk from Radcliff's bar on the corner of the Sand Mall and O'Dwyer's Bridge that crosses the Abbey River going from Athlunkard Street out to Corbally. Strangely enough the Cowhey family owned Radcliff's bar before they bought Angela Conway's public house. Angela Conway's public house is probably the best known in the Parish.

It often amazes me to know why a publican would change a famous well-established and internationally known name over a public house, just to see his own name over the door. It's like changing the famous name of Collin's Music Hall in London, and putting my name over it, or Jack Dempsey's famous Irish public house in New York, and putting a complete unknown name over it.

My local public house is W.J. South's in O'Connell Street, it is well known as a Limerick pub all over the world, and the best days work that the present proprietor David Hickey did was to retain the same name. Frank McCourt's book proved that, especially since the film Angela's Ashes was made, and showed the name over the door.

In my opinion the same applies to Angela Conway's bar, it will always be linked to the Tracy name in the Parrish and Limerick's famous packet and tripe.

Ever since I was a small child living in 8, Sir Harry's Mall with my Auntie May. I have some memories of one sort of another of Angela Conway's public house, especially around the Abbey Regatta time of year.

My first recollection of being in that pub was with my father as a very small boy. The front entrance to Angela's was facing the Abbey River, as you entered it would remind you of the old fashioned pubs when they used to sell groceries in the front part of the shop, and the bar was in the back. The main drinking area was in the back and the side door really became the most used door. It was also nearer to come in from the Arthluncard Street side, and Saint Mary's Church and of course Tracy's packet and tripe shop.

Angela's was a kind of stopping off place or waiting room for guys waiting to collect their orders from the famous Tracy's packet and tripe shop around the corner. There were a couple of nice souvenirs taken from the old timber bridge in the form of square timber beams about eighteen inches square cut to make stools about sixteen inches high off the floor.

You couldn't be in a more convenient spot if you wanted to watch the Abbey Regatta and hold a pint of Guinness in your hand at the same time. The two bars that done a roaring trade in the Parish when the Regatta was on were the ones in the Sand Mall Radcliff's Bar and Angela Conway's.

Radcliff's was the nearest pub to Pa Healy's field and it always did a good trade. The walls of the Abbey River as I remembered them on both sides, were a resting-place for seagulls some of them as big as albatrosses. If you followed the river around the corner bend in the

Sand Mall, and followed the wall as far as Barrington's Hospital. They spent every day perched on the walls ready to dive scavenging for any scraps oozing from the sewer pipes into the Abbey River.

My memories of what oozed from those pipes, was a constant flow of blood among other things. The blood came from the four meat factories in Limerick City constantly discharging the washing down, after the killings each day. The local butcher shops that did their own killing, I'm sure contributed to the constant flow of blood into the Abbey River also.

Fortunately I do have happy memories of what took place in the Abbey River at other times of the year. For instance the Abbey Regatta was something I looked forward to usually held on Sundays, when the meat factories and the seagulls had a rest day. There was an annual swim from Athlunkard Boat Club down the Abbey River under Baal's Bridge and Mathew Bridge out onto the Shannon River, finishing at Saint Michael's Boat Club. I spent many happy hours fishing with a bamboo fishing rod sitting on the wall facing the house where I lived with my Auntie May in 8, Sir Harry's Mall.

The house is since gone to make way for the new Abbey Bridge crossing the river at that point. To see the Guinness Barges shunting up and down the Abbey River to and from Troy's Lock laden with timber barrel's of Guinness, to be distributed throughout the City. The highlight of the Abbey Regatta was the greasy pole and duck race events. The duck race was a race where swimmers were invited to swim after a duck to try and catch it.

To my knowledge the only way this could be done, was to dive underwater and come up under the duck, trying to catch it by the legs. To see the crowds of men women and children sitting in picnic mood, eating ice cream bought in Peppers or O'Sullivans shop in the Irish Town or drinking lemonade bought from Angela Conway's Public

House. To see huge crowds all lining the walls of the Abbey River, and all in Carnival mood and the different make of boats being shown off by the Abbey Fishermen.

Most of those boats were made and decorated in beautiful colours by the fishermen themselves. There was always a carnival on in Pa Healy's field when the Regatta was on. It's hard to try to explain the feelings of pure joy I had living in the Sand Mall. Just sitting on the Abbey River wall fishing with a bamboo rod, beside real fishermen, is an experience I'll never forget.

Watching the Guinness barges loaded down with wooden barrels of Guinness shunting down the Abbey River, and manoeuvring their way through the floodgates into the canal at Troy's Lock, to be off loaded for delivery to the pubs in Limerick City. There seemed to be a shuttle service with Guinness barges coming and going from Limerick to Dublin.

Just think of the journey those sturdy Guinness barges loaded with timber kegs of Guinness manoeuvring through dozens of Canal Lock Gates, before it reached its final destination to enter the gates at Troy's Lock in Limerick City. I once saw a documentary on television where the famous Dick Warner made that trip negotiating those Lock Gates on that long trip from the Guinness Brewery at James's Gate in Dublin. The trip from Killaloe alone was fascinating and coming through the huge drop that had to be negotiated at the power station in Ardanchrusha, in order to get down to the level of the water in Killaloe, to continue it journey to the thirsty drinkers of Limerick and the surrounding areas.

As I already said ever since I was a small child living with my Auntie May in Sir Harry's Mall, from the Arthluncard boat club the activity that was going on in the Abbey River and the Canal holds lots of memories for me. Just looking at the men working in the cooperage and off loading the barrels of Guinness for delivery to the public houses in Limerick City and farther a field.

Another common sight I often saw was the river diver clad in his diving suit connected to his air hose going down the steel ladder into the water to clear away whatever was blocking the Lock gates from being fully opened. He looked like something from outer space with the copper helmet screwed on to his heavy leaded booted diving suit.

It never failed to amaze me to notice all the activity that used to go on in the canal area at that time. Between the Cooperage and the Guinness and the sand-cots bringing washed sand down from the Shannon River, the canal was a hive of industry. Horse and four-wheel carts were constantly being loaded up with Guinness for delivery to the local publicans.

The Guinness must have been good in those days, out of the old timber kegs, as it is today out of what they call the iron lung. To stand outside any public house in the Parish especially after the Abbey Regatta in those days, you wouldn't have to wait long to hear someone singing his head off, Angela Conway's public house was no exception, especially after a rugby match. All the good singers in the Parish could be heard singing in Angela Conway's at one time or another. Tracy's packet and tripe was always a good drawing plaster to get clients into Angela's public house also, God be with the old days

Chapter 18
Dick Devane's Bar

Dick Devane's bar as I knew it was situated on the corner of Arthluncard St. and Nicholas St., and is one of the well-known watering holes in the Parish. Most publicans had their own private secret way, of recognizing customers knocking to get in for drink, for the after hours trading. I remember a time when the pubs were only allowed to do business from 12-30pm to 2 o'clock and from five o'clock to seven o'clock pm on a Sunday evening. In order to get in after that time you needed to know the secret knock. It was a common sight to see guys waiting around corners for someone to come along, with the secret tapping that would get you in.

They were called knockers, and would usually get a pint from the guys that got them in. Each bar had a way of communicating with it's own customers, without taking a chance that a Civic Guard might be outside the door trying to make a raid, to catch illegal drinkers drinking after hours.

In some cases the publican had the knockers employed to get clients. And keep an eye on things that were happening out side the door after hours. They were later compensated with a few pints for their trouble. To my knowledge each area had their own way of working round those stupid early closing laws.

The law was very strict on drinking after hours. Not alone were the Publicans fined very heavy. But every individual in the bar that was caught was fined also. The Publicans also ran the risk of having had their licence endorsed. So much so that three strikes and they lost their licences. It was very important to keep on the right side of the law.

Some Publicans took big chances; I remember a saying going around about Dick Devane's bar at the corner of Nicholas Street and Arthluncard Street. A fellow customer was knocking outside Dick's pub on a Christmas night to get in. When Dick heard the knock he came to the door, but still kept it locked he then called out, "Who is there". Your man identified himself to Dick, then Dick said to him, "Who is with you," "No one said your man". Dick then shouted back to him, "Well go away and get a crowd".

While I'm on the subject of Dick Devane's public house, I heard one yarn about this young lad that had gone to England to work. He came from the Island Field in the Parish. He is supposed to have returned home for a holiday after less than one year working in London. He had a very strong cockney accent that was barely understandable. He decided to bring his mother and father into Dick Devan's public house for a drink, and to show off his newly acquired cockney accent.

It went something like this. When they entered the bar he sat his mother and father sitting down at the table inside the door. He then went up to the counter and asked Dick in a loud cockney voice to fill a pint of Guinness for himself. When Dick asked him what his father and mother was having, he turned round and asked his father, "What's the dolly girl having Pop". His mother answered, "I'll have a half pint of Guinness son". He then said to her, "And what's you soul mate having".

Having made a complete idiot of himself and embarrassed his parents. He asked Dick what number bus could he get to take them home to the Island Field. Bearing in mind that in those days there was no bus services to the Island Field ever. It used to amaze me to hear people talking a load of bull after being away for a couple of wet days and coming home with a swanky accent. For instance I remember going on a bus excursion out of Limerick with my father on what they used to call a mystery tour.

Those mystery tours would pick you up outside Cannock's store in O'Connell St. This particular summers night my father and I got on the bus, the fare was five shillings each. After a while the conductor came around to collect the fares. Most of the people on that bus would have known one another. When the conductor came up the bus to the seat in front of to take a young ladies fare. She asked him what the fare was, in a kind of bastard American accent at the same time holding out her hand with some loose change in it. He said, "five shillings miss".

She said to him, "Please take it, I don't understand this Irish money at all". My father started laughing and said to her, "Rita you must have a very short memory it's hardly twelve Months since you worked with me over in Cleeve's factory". That is the kind of bullshit I just couldn't understand from people that came home from England or the USA. Who did these people think they were fooling? You would stand a better chance of picking up one of those mock accents after visiting a film in the Tivoli or Thomond cinemas.

Dick Devan's public house was one of the great meeting places along with Angela Conway's Bar in the Sand Mall. The one thing that attracted guys to these public houses among other things was Tracy's

Packet and Tripe. They would place their orders for packet and tripe in Tracy's and more often than not they would have to wait till another batch was finished. There was so much demand for that delicacy that you may have to put your order in a couple of days in advance.

Packet and tripe was recommended by several doctors for people with stomach
Complaints. Hardened drinkers swore by it, they would tell you nothing could line your stomach better than a feed of packet and tripe. Each person had his or her own recipe for cooking it. The packet consisted of blood forced into a kind skin membrane just like a black or white pudding. It was sliced in rings the same as black pudding. The tripe was the belly of the sheep bleached white. To look at it was like looking at curly cabbage only it was bleached a creamy white colour.

When my father cooked it he cut the tripe into strips about one inch square, the packet was cut on rings about three quarters of an inch. It was first boiled in water with a pinch of salt until the tripe was tender. Then the water was drained off, and milk was added with chopped onion, pepper, and a knob of butter. This was brought back to the boil then left simmer for about one and a half hours on a low cooker setting, after that it was ready to eat either hot or cold.

They used to say you haven't lived if you haven't eaten Tracy's packet and tripe. Tracy's were famous several delicacies, I'm not sure if I should mention in this book one of those delicacies, but if I don't you will never know. The Reed was one part of the sheep's anatomy that was prized above all others by the connoisseurs of the packet tripe eaters union. The first time I ever heard it discussed was by my own brother Donal. When I asked him bluntly what was the reed he gently leaned over to me and whispered, "It's the sheep's arse hole".

Apart from pigs toes being sold in Tracy's they sold Sheep's feet they were called trotters. I remember when I lived in my Auntie May's house in Sir Harry's Mall, just around the corner from Tracy's and Angela Conway's public house. One of my jobs was to leave some dinner plated in to Tracy's on a Saturday night with my Aunts name on it with our regular order.

These plates would then be collected after Sunday Mass in St. Mary's Church in Arthluncard St. There was very little on the sheep's trotters they were just scraped and cooked then sliced in two, but with a dust of salt on them served cold they were pleasantly very grizzly but tasty to eat. I had very many happy memories living in the Sand Mall.

Chapter 19
Pinkie Downey's Bar

Pinkie Downey's bar was not an early morning market bar as it was outside the special boundary allocated for the market licence. But it was very near to the market area, it was situated at the bottom end of Bank Place the Street is now called Michael's street it was very close to the Abbey River in Charlotte Quay and the Granary; it has long since been demolished to make way for the new Limerick look as we know it today. Pinkies was a house of ill repute, it was a public house where women with black shawls hung out.

The idea was one or two rich farmers that wanted to try their hand at the wild side of life in Limerick city, and didn't like the idea of been seen in the dockland area, would visit Pinkie Downey's licensing establishment.

They would ply some prostitute in a black shawl, with plenty of drink. She could be an auld one, or a young one, and you probably wouldn't know that till you got her into bed. The saying was at that time that if you frequented Pinkie Downey's public house you had to go up stairs to get your change?

For the guys that liked to try their hand at a different form of getting thrills, they turned to gambling. There used to be a tossing school on waste ground that they called the cowl, just around the corner from Pinkie Downey's public house, and close to the old granary. This waste ground was directly at the back of the old sweet factory in Charlotte Quay, also known as the Assembly Mall.

Some of the most fearless gamblers in Ireland and as far away as England, and countries further a field, used this gambling site. Sailors off the boats always managed to find this gambling school. I suppose Pinkie Downey's house of ill repute had something to do with it also. I have seen farm animals, pony and traps, and even farms of land won and lost on the toss of two shiny halfpennies. This gambling site was run like a military operation, with lookouts and strong men to protect the wealthy men taking part in the gambling.

There was a snooker hall adjacent to the flat ground where the tossing took place. Polo Ryan was the guy that owned this establishment. It was also used as a clubhouse for Wembley rover's soccer team. On emergencies when rain stopped play, or the civic guards were on their way to make a raid. Some of the gamblers retreated to the sanctuary of the snooker hall, by the way playing snooker. But in fact turned to playing the serious gambling card games like brag or stud poker.

I have even heard but never witnessed, gypsies setting up bare fistfights, to bet on. A famous sporting journalist writing for an English newspaper called the Sunday People, once wrote about the calibre of the Irish gamblers in Limerick. He said they were pure lunatics and compared the things they did, to playing Russian roulette with their lives.

Then of course the more respectable gamblers frequented the dog track in the Markets Field to bet modestly on greyhound racing. That was a kind of safe bet in once sense, as the bookmakers were afraid to take on big bets. The limit with some bookmakers might be a five-pound note. If anyone rushed in with a bet any higher it was rubbed off the board immediately.

I often wondered how guys that had lost everything they had on two coins coped with their loss. It hurts me even today to think about that. I suppose they just signed them selves in to St Joseph's Mental Hospital and hoped the pain would go away. I just couldn't bear to think about their wives or families.

It wasn't uncommon to read in the local papers where some poor guy was fished out of the Shannon River, after loosing his life savings or worse still maybe his family home, in a tossing school. It doesn't bear thinking about what their families must have went through, for the greedy intentions of those foolish men trying to get rich quick. It's amazing how quick one guy could delight in seeing a poor bloke walking away without a penny left in his pocket.

On a lighter note, my grandfather used to work with the Limerick Corporation; one of his jobs was to open the public toilets at the top of William Street between 4 30 am and 5 o'clock on the early morning market days. This was done to accommodate the farmers coming into town. There was a horse trough positioned adjacent to the public toilets that was constantly used to give the horses water.

Bear in mind that most of the public houses in the area had licences to open their bar around the same time also. The bars that comes to my mind were The Munster Fair Tavern Bar, Jerry O'Deas Bar, Cahill's Bar, The Horse and Hound Bar, The Moose Bar, The Holy Ground Bar, The Gaelic Bar to name but a few.

Any morning of the working week those public houses were crowded. People came from miles around to visit those early morning premises. All for different reasons, mostly to get some kind of a cure before facing into work. Others might be waiting to get a call for to do casual work, from builders or farmers.

There were gangs of men coming off night work from the factories doing three cycle shifts. Krupps and Ferenka to name two, they were huge employers. Then the staff in St Joseph's Hospital and the Jail, and of course there was Shaw's meat factory, and McMahon's timber yard all big employers.

Limerick City was a hive of industry in those days the pay may not have been great but a lot of people were working. For instance all the hides, after the beasts were killed were taken from Shaw's, O'Maras, Mattersons, and Denny's meat factories to McCarthy's skin store in Cathedral Place to be scraped and prepared, then they were taken to O'Callaghan's Tannery in Gerald Griffin St. to be cured and turned into leather. The leather was transferred to the Shoe Factory to make boots and shoes. That was just one product and the whole process took place only a stone throw from one another.

There were hundreds of men and women working around the dockland area, and in places like Cleeve's factory, and the Flourmills, not forgetting the hundreds of Dockers unloading and loading cargo boats. There were hundreds of men and women working in Cleeve's factory alone. They made butter and cheese and powder milk they imported boatloads of tin. They had a special tin factory for making their own tins and exported cream and sweetened and unsweetened milk, and were world famous for the slabs of Cleeve's toffee they made.

They exported their food products all over Europe during the Second World War, and were huge employers of men and women. When the siren would go off as a signal to stop work, I often saw hundreds of men and women cycling home from work. My own father spent forty-eight years of his life working in Cleeve's factory.

Chapter 20

Nancy Blake's Bar

Nancy Blake's public house is situated in Denmark Street just around the corner from Chapel Lane and adjacent to Cruises Street It was next door to Clunes Tobacco factory long since demolished. I often frequented this public house especially on Saturday morning after visiting the milk market in Cornmarket Row a short distance away.

My first impression of Nancy Blake's bar was that it was a very cosy pub to have a drink in. As you entered the porch there was a door to your left that led into a front room lounge bar. The other door led into the back part of the pub that was the public bar. This room was one of the cosiest places you could wish to be in on a cold winters day. There was always a blazing fire on to greet you as you entered.

Many were the drink I had with my father in this little bar room. It was a regular meeting place to find friends after visiting the busy market. There was a barbershop facing the pub, and very often Nancy Blake's was used as a kind of second waiting room for guys wanting to have their haircut. Every now and again nipping over to see how many were in front of them. Nancy Blake was married to

Danny Mulcahy she still retained her own name over the pub.

I remember sitting at the bar in this public house talking to my father and couldn't help noticing one of the strangest sights I ever saw. It was a bunch of four-inch nails welded together and they were placed in an oval basket as if they had just been put there. Nancy Blake knew I was a carpenter and put the basket on the counter for me to see.

It transpired that she got them as a souvenir from one of the demolition workers employed to clear away the rubble, after the great fire that destroyed Newsom's hardware shop in William Street a short distance away. The steel girders were twisted and bent by the fierce heat, the complete premises was gutted. The heat was so intense that it welded the packet of four-inch nails together.

The front bar in Nancy Blake's was the place to go if you wanted to treat yourself to a bit of traditional Irish music. There was usually Irish music on a few nights each week and every weekend. It's amazing how the word gets around amongst the Irish music fanciers, it was always sure to fill Nancy Blake's public house. The fact that Nancy Blake's husband was a fluent Irish speaker may have something to do with it also.

The area outside the back door of the bar is a very nice and pleasant space to have a drink in on any time of the year. This area is where horses would have been stabled and the carriages stored in the old days. It is now used as a cold room for storing up to one hundred barrels of Guinness and beer. I know this from my son Michael who delivers Guinness to Nancy Blake's each week. The open space has a canopy that can be opened or closed at will.

It's more like something you would see in a Spanish resort. Looking through the old arch from the street entrance looks like a very inviting place to visit. Especially when you see couples sitting enjoying the excellent draught Guinness with creamy heads on the pints. It's also a place you can go to if the music of the occasional rock band gets to loud.

I was pleasantly surprised to read a pub spies comments about Nancy Blake's public house and the great Irish music that is played there every Thursday night. The web page was designed for the University of Limerick students union, giving them an insight into some of the traditional Irish music public houses in Limerick City. He concurred with my feelings about this very popular public house in the heart of Limerick City. He gave them a rating of four pints out of five and the nearest to excellent.

He made no reference to the excellent street markets adjacent to Nancy Blake's public house. Markets that brought donkey and carts into places like Mungret Lane. Carr Street Cornmarket Row, for decades of years longer than I can remember. Markets that today are still going strong. The only change that I can see is the donkey and cart gave way to Hiace vans and cars with trailers. Every Saturday morning the Milk Market attracts thousands of visitors looking for the weekly bargains in the line of garden vegetables. Everything from a pin to a computer is on sale in the Milk Market and those adjacent streets around it.

I can remember a time being led by the hand by my grandmother nearly sixty years ago. We walked from the Irish Town into Mungret Lane on our way to Cornmarket Row and the Milk Market; these streets were a hive of industry. Every small shop had some kind of business going. From blacksmiths, to cobblers, clay pipe makers, broom head makers, baskets makers, harness makers, to name but a few. Straw and hay could be bought in bales and oats for horses.

There was a shop on the corner of High Street and Cornmarket

Row called Feathery Bourke's. He was a scrap dealer and would buy feathers from the guys plucking the foul in the milk market. I often frequented him with bits of scrap from time to time to get money for the pictures. He would put it on the scales and give you what he thought it was worth.

Salted and fresh country butter, hen eggs and duck eggs, were on display on most donkey and carts small butter samples were available as tasters. Fowl was always plentiful with hen's ducks and geese for sale. The famous gardeners of Park had oceans of the vegetables on display; they were noted for the curly cabbages they grew. The whole atmosphere of the market gave it a kind of Christmas feeling.

The memories I have of the milk market are the beautiful aroma from the fruit on display. My grandmother ran a shop in Garryowen and used to buy apples by the barrel full. Old women wearing black shawls haggling over priced added to the atmosphere. For me there was never a dull day spent visiting that Saturday morning market. I have nothing more to add about Nancy Blake's bar, and my precious memories of the market days of old.

Chapter 21
Ma O'Leary's Bar

Ma O'Leary's public house was situated on the corner of Lady's Lane and Dominic Street. I'm glad to say this filthy excuse for a public house has long since been demolished and is no more. Mattersons bacon factory was on the opposite corner of the lane from the pub. I often wondered why anyone would frequent such a dirty smelly establishment. Once I had the most unpleasant visit to this dirty filthy public house.

I was surprised to learn from my father that quite a lot of very respectable guys frequented it for after hours drinking, even Government Ministers from time to time. Donough O'Malley was Minister for education and was one of her patrons along with several passed Lord Mayors of Limerick like Mossy Reidy, James Carew, and Dan Bourke to name but a few, Dan Bourke had his own public house a few doors up the street from Ma O'Leary's bar.

How they put up with drinking in this filthy bar I will never know. The glasses were just dipped into a bath of filthy water and filled straight away. Guys could have been eating pig's toes a few minutes before and drinking out of one of those glasses was surely a health hazard.

If it wasn't the smell of pigs coming from Mattersons factory drifting in, with the slightest breeze blowing the wrong way, it was from the piss hole in Ma O'Leary's toilet. The toilet in Ma O'Leary's was in the basement and was very badly lit. The bulb for some reason was always missing. I suppose undesirable customers were always knocking it off.

As a result most guys when they wanted to make a piss they

left it go at the door at the top of the stairs. Anyone that had the misfortune to spend a penny down below, ran the risk of getting something they didn't expect. It wasn't uncommon to hear a guy call out, "Coming up".

Unfortunately I witnessed a man that had gone down to spend a penny dressed in his Sunday best, only to get the full contents of a Gawker's stomach on the way up. He was like a fellow that was after being pebble dashed. I knew that man and he left that public house completely destroyed. As far as I know that man took the pledge and he never darkened a public house, or touched alcoholic drink for the rest of his entire life.

There were so many jokes going around Limerick at the time about guys that got the "trots" from drinking bad porter. I was once told about a man that was suffering with a very bad dose of the trots or runs. He went to the Dispensary to see a doctor to see if he could help him. The Doctor is supposed to have given the man three pence to go to Mattie Boland's shop beside the Dispensary in Gerald Griffin Street to get a packet of bisto gravy.

He was told to take two good spoonfuls and mix it with some water and that he would be all right. Poor man went and got the bisto, and was thinking to him self what that would do for him. So he decided to go back to ask the Doctor. The Doctor told him if it done nothing else it, might help to thicken it up for him. Stories like that were all right to laugh at, but it was no joke to be on the receiving end of one of those wicket mean publicans.

The smell out of some of the toilets after a guy that had to run after drinking a bad pint of Guinness was something else. It often sent other guys running to the loo with what they used to call the gawks. The Gawks was another kind of sickness that had to be cured, and the only sure way to get cured was to come back for more of what made you sick in the first place.

For instance if you had a session of drink the day before, then went home to have a feed then sleep it off. The Guinness started to ferment for the second time in your stomach with what ever you ate, resulting in a severe cramp in your tummy as a result of a build-up of acid. This acid has to be got rid of one way or another.

The one sure way is to return to the pub and ask for a curer. In the hope that you didn't get another Mickey fin in the form of a bad pint of porter, and making sure to sit on your own, very near to a toilet. It is very important to get a good pint of Guinness to sip slowly when you are nursing a dose of the Gawks. If you happened to get a dodgy one you could be in big trouble, if you have to run to the jacks. You won't know which end you are using to get rid of the Gawks. More often than not you will shit in your trousers, and puke all over your self at the same time.

A lot of the farmers visiting Limerick City knew this bad pints practice was going on, and only drank from bottles that they could see being opened in front of them. The trade the farmers brought in spilled out around the City of Limerick far and wide. After all the business of buying and selling was done. The farmers and travellers turned their intentions to a bit of entertainment; some had other ideas like sowing their seed in houses of ill repute in Limerick City. The ladies of the night plying their trade selling their bodies to the rednecks could be seen parading the dockland areas in large groups after dark.

The local caf 's were always full of potential customers for to keep the ladies going. I remember one local draper telling me years after; he sold dozens of pairs of under wear to the prostitutes operating in the dock land area. He just couldn't keep the ladies of the night supplied with panties, as all their clients wanted to take home some souvenirs, to remind them of their day out in Limerick.

Each client was invited to take off the souvenir for himself and put it in his pocket. As soon as the client was satisfied and had his trophy to take home, the lady replaced the garment with another. That process was repeated over and over, needless to say the local draper was well satisfied also.

Chapter 22
Charlie St. George's Bar

Charlie St. George's public house is located in number 41, Parnell St. its almost facing Colbert Railway Station in Limerick City. If ever a public house had a tradition for supporters following a rugby team it is this public house. Young Munster is not just a rugby team they are a religion it this public house and always was. Even though the pub is at the wrong side of the Monument. The Young Munster supporters always boast of being at the back of the Monument. The Brother Rice Monument in the peoples park is where this monument can be found. The yellow road is in the heartland of the Young Munster territory.

Some of their Indians can be found, as far up as Waller's well, and Janesborough you couldn't miss them when they are on the warpath. They are usually painted in their black and amber war paint colours. The best example of one of their chiefs I describe in chapter 4 of this book. But seeing as I'm telling a story about one of their favourite watering holes Charlie St. Georges bar, it's worth another mention. Of course Dollars Mulcahy in his hey day could be called one of Young Munster's famous supporters.

But there was a woman who lived in Reeve's Path that had a

rake of old mongrel dogs. She dressed them up in the black and amber colours and wheeled them in a pram out to Thomond Park when Young Munster's were in action. I remember a Priest from St. Josephs Parish his name was Fr. Harry Began. He slept ate and drank Young Munster. He talked of nothing else only rugby in the rugby season, and never failed to mention his favourite Young Munster team and even asked the people to pray for them from the alter. Father Harry as he was called had only three hobbies, forgiving sins, rugby, and golf in that order.

One of Limerick's greatest sons was a Young Munster man, and was picked and played for Munster as far back as 1948. Every time he visited Limerick he rarely ever missed keeping in touch with his friends and was a regular visitor to Charlie St. George's public house, he loved to be in the company of his Young Munster friends. I was told a story about the time Richard Harris played rugby for Old Crescent and Garryowen. It seems he spent some time in the Sanatorium in St. Camillus's Hospital and never had a visit from any of his teammates; the only rugby players that came to visit him were Young Munster players.

He never forgot that and as soon as he recovered from his illness he signed up with Young Munster, the rest is history. It's ironic that I only started to write this book about three weeks before Richard Harris died in a Chelsea hospital in London. I once met him in Kempton Park racetrack at a night meeting in the nineteen sixties. I happened to back one of his two-year-old fillies that came in second and I lost a tanner into the bargain. Richard at that time was on his way up and as usual had a beautiful dolly bird hanging out of his arm.

Richard Harris was a brilliant actor and film star as everyone knows. He made a black and white film where he was playing the part of a rugby player; it was called, "The sporting life". He was a natural of course to play this part, and they say he should have got an "Oscar for the part he played in it". I don't suppose there is a Limerick person that wasn't proud to see him on the big screen in our cinemas in Limerick City. To my knowledge he always got to play the good guy in his films, and I don't ever remember him to change his accent. He must have been an inspiration for anyone that performed on the humble stage in the Crescent Hall in O'Connell Street here in Limerick, where he first learned his trade acting.

I was overjoyed when Russell Crowe the famous Canadian actor and film star (my own favourite actor by the way), took time off to attend his funeral in London. I remember Richard Harris saying in a recent television interview, that Russell Crowe asked him to sell the Munster jersey he won in 1948. Richard Harris said, "It was so precious to him, he wouldn't sell it for a million pounds".

After the funeral in London Russell Crowe paid a visit to Limerick and found his way to Charlie St. George's public house, I can imagine him trying to get the feel, of what Richard Harris must have felt, just looking at the old photographs in this famous public house. I'm sure that Richard Harris would have told him about the no hoper's famous victory over Lansdowne, and bringing the cup home to Limerick City, when Young Munster won the Bateman Cup on the 14th April 1928, including the joke going around that they told no one about it.

I can imagine him recalling the stories Richard Harris would have told him about the famous characters as he glanced over the old photographs hanging on the wall in the pub. Looking at guys like Charlie St. George, and Danaher Sheehan, and all the rest of the famous names associated with the Bateman Cup victory. Most of those players came from the back of the Monument. Danaher Sheehan's right name was Michael Sheehan but his mother's maiden name was Danaher, so he went by the name Danaher Sheehan. He lived in Halls Range in Edward St. beside Murphy's public house and facing Sarsfield Barracks.

I'm open for contradiction but I barely remember my father telling me a story about the Bateman Cup. It seems an Englishman by the name of Bateman, who ran a Carnival on the grounds of where St Joseph's Church now stands in O'Connell St donated it. When Young Munster won it in 1928, he told me they were lighting tar barrels and bonfires in all the lanes and streets at the back of the Monument, from the Yellow Road to Waller's Well. The bombing field known today as Caledonian Park was a great place for lighting bonfires. The bombing field got its name from the British Army using it to detonate explosives.

To get back to one of Limerick cities greatest sons, there was another side to Richard Harris, the one where he and his buddies were full of devilment. I remember I was once in the Savoy cinema in Limerick and I witnessed some of the tricks Richard Harris and his buddies got up to, this is long before he became an actor. It was no bother for him and his pals to piss up into the air in the cinema for a laugh, or out over the balcony in the God's in the Lyric or Tivoli cinemas.

Tossing lighted cigarette buts down into the audience was another trick of his. Another trick he was known to have pulled was he would ask the guy behind him for a light from his cigarette. When he got it he would break the cigarette in two, then light the other end, and give it to someone else to hand it back, to the poor guy that gave it to him in the first place. There were the poor blokes kicked out of the pictures over him and the tricks he got up to.

Richard Harris had one of many friends that he kept in touch with ever since he left Ireland, to make his fortune on stage and in films. For the life of me I don't know why. This man shall remain nameless he was another crazy guy like Harris. I once saw him in a public house, not in Charlie St. George's I might add, and he was well loaded up with Guinness. This guy was told to go home he had enough but insisted on getting another drink. He took out a wad of pound notes; he had more money than sense and started to light one of them in the ashtray, to the astonishment of the proprietor. So much so that the proprietor relented, but said he would only give him a tomato juice.

Your man tipped the tomato juice into his pint glass and mixed it with what was left of his pint. Then he threw back his throat and made for the front door. He pebbled dashed the back of the front door before he had a chance to reach the street. The mistake he made was he forgot he was in Bull Hayes's public house in Clontarf Place, just off O'Connell St. Bull jumped out over the counter and caught your man by the collar and the scruff of the arse and through him straight out the door, giving him a kick up in the arse at the same time. Needless to say he was never served again in that bar. He was one of those guys that just didn't know when to stop; hopefully he saw the error of his ways when Bull Hayes had sorted him out.

To end on a happy note I was delighted to read in our local newspaper the Limerick Leader that it's being suggested that Richard Harris is to be awarded the freedom of our city posthumously. It should have been given to him when he was alive, but better late than never. I called to W.J. South's bar the morning before the Saturday morning I attended Richard Harris's Mass funera.l I met a great Young Munster player in his day his nickname was Dollars Mulcahy he was having a small drop of the creator before he went into the Church, he rose his glass to me to salute the memory of his old buddy Richard Harris. I asked him if he was going to the funeral? The answer he gave me was, "Why wouldn't I? Sure he's one of our own isn't he". "

I asked him if he thought there would be enough room to get into the funeral Mass".

He said, "There will always be room for a Young Munster man anywhere in this town, pointing to the crest on his tie and tapping the larger one on his blazer". I asked him if he had seen Sash Conway around, I knew Richard Harris always tried to meet up with Sash every time he came to Limerick. Dollars told me Sash had married a Spanish girl and was living in Spain.

I thanked him for the information he gave to me and made my way to the Church. When the service was over, I made my escape as soon as I could, away from the huge crowd to get some money from cash point in the nearby bank two blocks away. About fifteen minutes later I was walking up O'Connell St. I spotted Sash Conway linking his first cousin who appeared to be having difficulty in walking. I decided not to bother them and left them go.

There was one sure thing I knew they were heading off to some nearby but well-established watering hole, to possibly meet some more friends of Richard Harris, and down a couple of the top shelf specialities, to toast the wonderful memories of one of Limericks favourite sons. At the same time remembering how it used to be.

Richard Harris was born in Limerick City on 1st October 1930 and died on 25th October 2002 in London, above are his final written words before he died, reprinted on the back of the Mass booklet I received when I attended his Mass at the Jesuit Church here in Limerick City on Saturday 30th November 2002 at 11 o'clock, it reads:

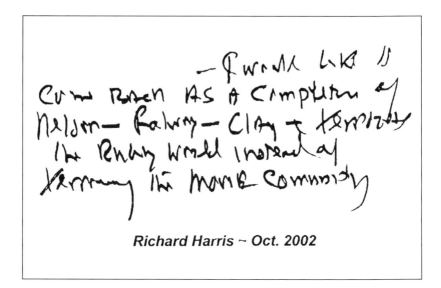

Richard Harris ~ Oct. 2002

"I WOULD LIKE TO COME BACK AS A COMPILATION OF NELSON, GALWEY AND THE CLAW, AND TERRIFY THE RUGBY WORLD INSTEAD OF THE MOVIE COMMUNITY"

I have no doubt he is probably with all those rugby greats that he played against, and the ones he was told about in places like Charlie St Georges public house, among the many pubs that he frequented in his lifetime. On Saturday 18th January 2003, Munster made history by beating Gloucester by four tries and twenty-seven points to six in Thomond Park. That day history was made in the rugby world. They say Richard Harris had something to do with it from the other side of the spirit world. May he rest in peace?

Chapter 23
Walter Hurley's Bar

Walter Hurley's bar was facing the Kiosk that is built into the Peoples Park after crossing the railway station and Reeve's Path on your way up to Edward St.

There was a maze of little lanes at the back of his public house. Dixon's Lane was probably the most well known of all those lanes in the area. Of course just around the corner, was the famous Carey's Road otherwise known as the Yellow Road. Big changes have taken place since the demolition of the lanes in Limerick. There is an open space and a spacious green where Walter Hurley's pub once stood surrounded by some of the most famous lanes of Limerick City.

I remember drinking in Walter Hurley's public house one Sunday night with several of my new friends that I had teamed up with since leaving Sarsfield Avenue, in Garryowen, to live in Emmett Place just a short walk away. My new friends used to frequent this particular pub because the proprietor allowed them to play cards for money after hours. Bear in mind all the public houses used to close at 7pm on Sundays.

My usual drink was Bulmers Cider with a dash of raspberry in it; you could get a pint of cider for one shilling and three pence in those days. My friend William Dennehy and I would buy an unopened quart bottle of cider between us for a half crown, and get two half-pint glasses to drink it the raspberry was free.

We would go to Walter Hurley's pub about 8pm; it was a great meeting place to have a drink to get a bit of Dutch courage before heading off for one of the dance halls in the City. St Johns Pavilion was where you went for the Ceili dancing, two shillings was the entrance fee.

The Stella Ballroom was the place to go for English dancing, the prices varied from two shillings to a half crown. The National, The Royal George, The Glentworth, and Cruises were all hotels that catered for dancing. Other dancehalls that comes to mind were St. Michaels in Cecil St. and the Connolly Hall was in Sarsfield St.

The prices varied in all those places depending on the bands that were playing. The cheapest dance hall and one of the best was a place called Toddies. It was over in Mary St. the dance hall was in the same building as St. Mary's band room. The only fault with it was the crowds were big and the dance hall small.

I was drinking in Walter Hurley's pub one Sunday night with the boys, when a knock came to the door. Two men came in I could barely make out the shapes of their silhouettes in the candlelight. Its only when they spoke I got the fright of my life. One of the men was my own father. I just didn't know what to do; I felt if he found me in a public house especially after hours he would have killed me.

Fortunately the bar was so badly lit just a few candles lighting the card tables, otherwise the bar was pitch black. I knew I had to get out of that pub before my father found out I was in there. I went out to the toilet to check if there was any way out, the light was still very bad fortunately for me. When to my horror the door opened and the next thing I noticed a man standing beside me relieving himself. He said, " Not a bad night boss". I hesitated and was about to mumble, suddenly another guy answered, " It's great thank God for this time of year".

While that conversation was going on I walked away and made my escape to the far end of the bar to be near the front door, my mates were covering me at this stage. I noticed a man that lived in Emmett Place, his name was Jimmy O'Hagan he was a train driver, but worst still he had a good look at me, I knew he knew who I was. All I could hope for was that he didn't get talking to my father and tell him I was in the bar. Jimmy O'Hagans wife was Anne Kelly they had two daughters Rita and Kitty. Kitty was the same age as me. I remember her telling me her mother's brother used to live in our house, before we move in to Emmett Place. I remember thinking to myself, I must tell her to tell her father not to ever mention that he saw me in Walter Hurley's public house.

Suddenly my prayers were answered somebody was caught cheating with the cards. Then all hell broke loose then Walter Hurley opened the door to let everyone out, I was the first and you wouldn't see my heel for dust, until I was well out of sight. That's one experience I had and will never forget in after hours public house drinking.

That was usually a quite public house, but every now and again trouble would break out. I remember another time being in there drinking in the dark when one guy threw a pint of Guinness over another fellow. It seems there was a bit of jealousy going on over Walter Hurley's daughter and two suitors, who happened to be trying to make a date with her. One of the guys was after getting a new suit of clothes made in Burtons.

Naturally he looked dressed to kill, so much so that the other guy got jealous and the first chance he got in the badly lit pub to show his anger he drowned poor man with his own pint of Guinness. That row went on for weeks every time the two guys met they belted one another. The only good thing to come out of that episode was, the guy that got the Guinness poured over him got the girl, and eventually they got married.

The Lanes of Limerick City as I remembered then in those days were the place to settle arguments. Especially after closing times in public houses the same would apply to when the dances were over. Guys fought over girls in dance halls quite a lot; this usually spilled out on the street or was taken down a lane to be settled. Usually they shook hands at the end of the fight until the next time.

The worst kind of fighting I ever witnessed, was over one of the most beautiful girls I ever saw. She happened be in a family of all brothers, the problem she had no matter what guy asked her home from the dance, that poor guy had to contend with taking on her brothers. If poor man happened to get the better of the argument he had to take on the whole of her family.

I have seen terrible fights over that lovely girl and her mad family of brothers. Eventually she had to immigrate to England to try and make a life for herself. She had no hope of finding a man in Limerick, and no one would even take her up for a dance for fear of been asked out to fight, by one of her lunatic brothers. I often watched the Civic Guards going into action breaking up fighting in the streets.

They showed no mercy, belting guys into the police barracks. There was one Guarda Sergeant in particular that stands out in my memory his name was Sergeant Harran. He was in charge of John Street Barracks down in the Irish Town. Every Friday and Saturday night it was no trouble to see him and a few more policemen belting up to a dozen guys into that police station. He made them pay for calling him out. They would be black and blue before the ever appeared in the courthouse.

One would have to be a bit of a hard man to join the police force in those days. I often went down the Irish Town with my friends on a Friday night; we often went to Donkey Fords for chips. The guard's barracks was a bit further down. As I already said it was a common sight to see drunken men being pushed into the police station for fighting, when they were crazy from drink. I remember the guards beating the drunks into the police station with batons. That thing used to go on every Friday or Saturday night regularly. Sometimes we would be coming from the Thomond cinema and the same thing would be happening, in Mary St. police station.

I often wondered, as a little boy growing up, how those drunken men could do what they did in those times, and then face into work the following morning as if nothing had happened. They didn't seem to care for anyone or anything only themselves. How some of them got a woman to live with them, I will never understand till the day I die. Those men made life very hard and miserable for everyone around them. The policemen of Limerick City earned their wages in those bad old days, and that's for sure.

Chapter 24
Charlie Malone's Bar

Charlie Malone's bar is situated on the corner of Wolfe Tone Street and Bowman Street, and is facing the famous Barrack Hill, where the Irish American Frank McCourt lived with his family. Frank McCourt made Limerick famous for a different reason and for the book he wrote called "Angela's Ashes" later made into a film. I have no doubt that Frank McCourt's father being a drunkard if we believe what he wrote in his book. Must surely have frequented this pub that I'm about to write about. Even though it has changed hands it still has Charlie Malone's name over the door

My first recollection of Charlie Malone's public house was around the time Sean South was killed in the North of Ireland. My father used to drink in his pub and was a regular customer of his. I only went to the pub to meet my father to get my weekly allowance. It wasn't much to look at as you entered the front door there was a snug on your left that could seat about four people. This area was strictly for women that used the bar. It was unheard of for women to sit in the public bar in those days.

The wooden counter at the front of the bar as you walked in

was only about three foot high, it was originally built when public houses, used to sell groceries at the front counter and drink at the back, and were called half way houses. Charlie used to sit at the low counter looking out the front window for potential customers coming down Barrack Hill. Most of Charlie's customers were Irish Free State soldiers.

The back gate in Barrack Hill was the gate the Army lorries and soldiers used to enter and leave Sarsfield Barracks in those days. On paydays whatever time the soldiers finished Charlie Malone's bar was usually the first port of call to settle the book for outstanding bill for drink.

Quite a few men that worked in the dockland area used Charlie's public house. Places like Ranks Mill and the McMahon's timber yards and Dockers unloading ships. My father used to bring his friends that worked in Cleeve's factory up to Charlie's. Bearing in mind the pubs used to close at seven o'clock on Sunday nights. In the summer season my father worked seven days a week on twelve hour shifts, after finishing work himself and his mates would polish off a barrel of Guinness in a couple of hours no bother.

My father liked Charlie Malone's, because you could get a drink after hours. Sunday night the pubs opened from five to seven o'clock p.m. He often worked late on Sundays in the summer time and Charlie knew that. They had a special knock worked out between them. Whatever time my father finished it was no trouble for him to get in for a drink. He often brought lots of his friends to Charlie's; Charlie's was a great meeting place.

I met a friend of mine one night in Charlie Malone's pub. His name was Gerry Lillis he lived three doors away from where the famous Frank McCourt's mother lived, in Little Barrington Street. My house was just two minutes walk from Gerry Lillis's house. Gerry asked me if I would be interested in going out with him on a blind date. Gerry said the girl he had a date with, had a friend, and she told him she wouldn't go, unless her friend was going also. I said I didn't mind, as girls never entered my head until that fateful night.

The arrangement was we were to meet them at a Ceili dance in the Connolly Hall, and see them home after the dance. Gerry Lillis's date was a girl called Noreen Collins, from a place called Mountcollins, in Abbeyfeale in County Limerick. The girl I was matched up with was called Mary Graham she came from Patrick's Well, County Limerick. Both of them were working and living in the staff quarters, in the Regional Hospital. When the dance ended we walked the two girls as far as the hospital gate. After some kissing and cuddling and it was time to go home.

Noreen Collins asked me if I would go to the Red-Cross dance, in the Stella Ballroom, the following Thursday night. She said she would be looking out for me if I went there. That is the first time I knew she took a fancy to me. I must admit I felt the same about her. I told her I would let her know and we left it at that. After I left her I just couldn't get her out of my mind.

I made my mind up to see her again so I phoned her shortly after I first met her at the Regional Hospital, and asked her if she would like to go to the pictures with me the following Thursday night. She said she would love to, I agreed to meet her at the bus stop outside Bernard Greens clothes shop in O'Connell Avenue. I intended to bring Noreen to my house in Emmett Place first, and then take her to the pictures afterwards.

I had met a man by the name of Paddy Ryan, In Charlie's the night after I first met Noreen Collins. This man was a great friend of my father. It turned out that he was the head Porter in the Regional Hospital and he lived in the gatehouse lodge at the main gate as you entered the hospital. Paddy Ryan knew everyone working in the hospital, better still he knew all about them and where they came from. I asked Paddy if he could find out about a girl called Noreen Collins.

He said he would and if I called into the pub the following night, he would let me know. The next night Paddy Ryan told me Noreen Collins was from a place called Cahirhayes, about one mile from a place called Mount Collins, in Abbeyfeale, County Limerick. He also told me she had a sister Kathleen working with her. He said they were both living in the hospital, and were fed and found, and paid ten pounds per Month. He said she must have had great pull in her family, to get two members of the same family, working in the newly opened Regional Hospital in Limerick City.

I paid the barman for four pints, two for Paddy Ryan and two for my father. I was delighted to hear what I had been told. I was looking forward to meeting Noreen on Thursday night. The more I was thinking about her, the more I wanted to get to know her. I met her as arranged off the bus, in O'Connell Avenue. I walked her as far as Emmett Place, and showed her the house where I lived in number 5. I told her we didn't have the time to go in, if we wanted to see the start of the film.

I took her to see a film in the Royal Cinema called "High Society." Grace Kelly and Bing Crosby sang a song in the film called "True Love." I'll never forget a scene in the film, where the two of them sang that song on a boat. I knew I was jumping the gun a little bit. But it said exactly how I felt about Noreen Collins, at that moment in time. I put my arm around her and said to her, "this is a beautiful love song isn't it Noreen." She agreed, and when Bing sang, "I'll give to you what you give to me true love true love". All the couples in the cinema seemed to move closer together and started to cuddle. I was no exception and pulled Noreen closer to me then we kissed. From that day on, any time I hear that song, I think of the first night I kissed Noreen Collins.

I made it my business to meet Noreen every time she was off and able to meet me, even if she was only off for a few hours some evenings. We took in every dance hall in Limerick City, and a few more pictures I loved being in her company.

Noreen could not get over how I managed to know so much about her. She was choked when I told her that she came from a place called Cahirhayes in Abbeyfeale. When I asked her how her sister Kathleen was. She looked at me as if I had two heads. She spent the night trying to find out how I knew what I did.

I finally told her about Paddy Ryan, and mentioned everything he told me about her. She said, "wait till I get my hands on him." Then she burst out laughing and said she couldn't wait to tell her sister Kathleen about it.

I had plans to go to London to work around that time to find work. I asked Noreen if she would consider being my steady girlfriend she said yes. The rest is history, I married her the same year she had our first son Christopher who was born in the Bedford Row Hospital in Limerick. I happened to be in Charlie Malone's public house when the news came that my wife Noreen gave birth to a baby boy.

Charlie gave me a glass of Brandy with a drop of Port wine in it and said to me, clasping my hand in a vicelike grip and said, "That you may be the father of a Bishop O'Donovan". So I have good cause to remember Charlie Malone and his public house that of course was back in 1958. Since I returned home to Ireland to live with my wife and four sons in 1970. My good friend Charlie Malone had passed away and his good wife Mrs Malone ran the bar for a time. When she retired it was run by her daughter Miriam and son-in-law Jim Culhane.

I had known Miriam and her brothers ever since they were little nippers, now it was strange to be served by Charlie's daughter and son-in-law, Jim Culhane. If I may say the atmosphere in that public house never changed. I recognised several of the old faces that were around in Charlie's time. But I'm sad to say that most of the old characters that I had known weren't around anymore. The snug and the old counter was gone, all the new improvements I must say Charlie would have approved of. The ground floor of the bar was made bigger as a result of moving the kitchen in Charlie's time up stairs. There was much more space in the bar since those renovations were carried out.

Charlie Malone's bar was one of the first few bars that I ever drank in after hours in the old days. Bars have come a long way since those times. Today the only way to experience the feelings we used to have, is to get into a public house on a Christmas morning or Good Friday. I won't mention where these pubs are I'll leave that up to you. I'm sure there is a few left, if not there are plenty of legal premises like the Rugby Clubs, Drapers Club, C.I.E Club, and I believe the Army Barracks.

But you haven't lived until you've heard a knock at a public house door, when your in there after hours on say a Good Friday, or Christmas morning or night, that's when the secret knock is most effective. At least you know it isn't a Copper waiting outside ready to knick you, but the fear of not knowing makes for exciting drinking, and looking at the anxious faces of your friends, adds to the thrill of knowing that you are breaking the law and hopefully you are going to get away with it.

Charlie Malone's is now under new management, Pat Kelly from Kilmallock County Limerick is the new man. He obliged the residents of Emmett Place to a great treat, and made everyone welcome on out annual get-together, at the back end of his roomy public house. Pats father owns Bulgadin Castle in Kilmallock and it was him that supplied our finger licking grub free of charge I might add, that seem to be a regular daily treat for anyone frequenting Charlie Malone's Bar. I'm glad to say Pat told me he intends to retain Charlie's Malone's name over the door.

Around Christmas time the card games played for turkeys or hams are the big attraction in Charlie Malone's bar. One of the best forty-five card players I ever had the privilege to observe playing, or even better still to partner in a good game of forty-five, is a man called Mick Cannon. Mick has been frequenting Charlie's for donkey's years, and I rate him as part of the furniture. As a matter of fact the last time I was in Charlie's, I was pleasantly surprised to see a framed monochrome photograph, of Mick Cannon and the young proprietor Pat Kelly.

They appeared to be looking back at me from the pride of place on the wall. It is also positioned facing the most favoured position to observed the card players in operation; I couldn't help thinking that the Cannons watchful eyes were keeping tract of every move the card players were making.

Chapter 25
The Wolfe Tone Bar

The Wolfe Tone bar is situated on the corner of Wolfe Tone Street and O'Connell Avenue. For the amount of times I frequented this public house, I found it a fairly cosy and comfortable place to have a drink in. Apart from one regular bar man and some part timers serving inside the counter, it's more or less a family run public house. The proprietors name is Bobby Byrne he was a former Fine Gael Mayor of Limerick City on a few occasions.

The Wolfe Tone bar has been in the Byrne family for the best part of fifty years. Bobby's wife Helen was the one I mostly saw serving inside the counter any time I happened to go in there. The residents of Emmett Place where I happen to live, often held their annual get together in the back room and the bar of Bobby Byrne's public house. Many happy nights were spent in conversation getting to know our new neighbours on those annual meetings.

Bobby Byrne is well known for his fundraising charities such as holding coffee morning get togethers, and providing his premises for holding Monthly Church fund draws, to raise badly needed funds for the restoration of our Parish Church St Josephs in O'Connell Avenue.

Bobby's daughter Maria is following in her father's footsteps, as she is an active Fine Gael city councillor, and deputy Mayor of Limerick City. I have often seen her dressed in her city council robes, and wearing the deputy Mayoral chain of office, standing in for John Cronin our city Mayor. When the family public house is busy she also gives a hand inside the counter.

I have known many of the regular patrons down through the years that frequented The Wolfe Tone Bar. They came from Wolfe Tone Street and the avenues around it. Famous tradesmen especially the painter and letter writing painter families like, the Dillon's and McAteers and the Roaches. To view a small sample of the painting work done by Charlie Roach, look up on the gable end wall of the Wolfe Tone Bar.

There was always a very good local clientele frequenting Bobby Byrnes public house. I remember droves of men on their way home from their place of work in the Limerick dockland area. They either came from Ranks Mill or McMahon's Timber yards, and the hundreds of Dockers that worked on the boats. The Wolfe Tone Bar got a fairly good share of that work force, on their way home from work.

Chapel nights for men attending the Holy Family Confraternity three nights per week, or when Missions were on, usually got its fair share of the spill over from the huge crowds attending. A number of the local Choirs and the Boherbuoy Band regularly relax in the back lounge, and a great nights entertainment usually ensues with much singing and crack.

The Wolfe Tone Bar trade has developed over the past number of years, and nowadays many people go to Bobby Byrnes for their lunch, apart from catering for christenings, weddings, and funeral. The social gatherings that take place in this establishment are many, like student meeting for quick lunch breaks and the usual office parties, from the many offices around the locality.

On big events like match days people stop off at Bobby's for a sandwich on their way to the match, or some post match analysis after the game. Rugby is a very popular sport in the bar, and on many occasions Limericks Keith Wood could be seen pulling the occasional pint before he became an international rugby player.

I have it on good authority that John Mitchell; trainer manager of the All Black Rugby Team lunched in the Bar in the past, and our very own Paddy Reid, of Rugby Grand Slam Fame is a great friend of all the Byrnes. Bobby has accumulated pictures of all the teams who have won the AIB All Ireland League, on a special wall in the Bar. His most recent addition to the collection was the photograph of the Dungannon Team, which makes it a truly All Ireland Collection.

The Bateman Tour visits Bobby's every year. This tour usually takes place after a home game, and the feast of the day is Limericks own world famous packet and tripe. Helen cooks this beautifully, and it is well washed down with Guinness. Many a Doctor in Limerick would have recommended a feed of Tracy's packet and tripe to settle a queasy stomach, after a feed of Guinness. I remember visiting the Savoy Cinema restaurant in the Bedford Row, to have a feed of tripe and mash on a Saturday night after dancing for three or four hours. One shilling and three pence was the price of it in those days.

Being a Limerick man Bobby and his family have a great love for all sports, and attend the entire Limerick hurling matches. Many heated debates have been held when the Limerick team is being selected, especially when an occasional selector dropped in for a quiet pint! The Ballinacurra Gaels hold their meetings in the back lounge, of the Wolfe Tone Bar and regularly organise fundraisers their The Limerick Super League Basketball Team are regular visitors to the Wolfe Tone Bar, and recently won the Men's ESB Cup.

Every Wednesday night Summerville Rovers hold their weekly draw in the bar and also hold table quizzes to raise funds towards their new clubhouse. Bobby's are regular participants in the inter pub soccer competition, and a photograph hangs on the wall of the winning team.

One very successful night held annually is the Art Exhibition. This event usually raises money for local charities, and features well known artists from the Raheen Studio Group. Most of the paintings are sold on the night, though one or two will sell in the days afterwards they usually auction one painting. As you can imagine, the regular news of the day is always a topic for debate in Bobby's.

One other distinction that can be attributed to Bobby Byrne is he had the pleasure of presenting the Freedom of Limerick City to Pope John Paul 11, the Papal Nuncio Allibrandi, and Bishop Jeremiah Newman in 1979, when the Pope visited Green park Racecourse during his Irish visit in 1979.

Chapter 26

Eric's Bar

Eric's Public house is situated on the corner of Emmett Place, and is in 42, St Joseph St. It is once more under new management by two young lads and they like to be known as Gerry Heddigan and Eddie Fraher, these two lads run a very orderly public house and will go a long way in my opinion. I first knew this pub as Stephen Coughlan's.

My first encounter of visiting this public house was as far back as 1951, that's the year our family moved to Emmett Place, to live. The bar in those days was one big square room that had a small snug. As you entered the front door, there were a couple of divisions dividing up the counter that gave a little privacy for small groups to have a chat. Of course the snug was one of those places if there were women in the group.

I remember the different guys that ran that pub from time to time, had a problem with the window display bottles, being knocked off by women wearing black shawls that drank in the snug. Imitation bottles of Paddy or Power whiskey were constantly being stolen by auld ones thinking they were the real thing, but in fact were only coloured water dummies. All they had to do was slide open the glass panel doors to get access to the front window display. There were lots of traps set, to doctor the coloured water in those mock bottles of whiskey.

I remember Charlie Malone telling me once; he put some sort of a laxative in the bottles and hoped it would do the trick, to stop the bottles being stolen from the window. Those bottles looked so real, it was hard to blame some auld one from the temptation of stealing them. Most publicans used to bottle their own whiskey and bottle the stout in the early days.

I remember finding a nest of miniature empty whiskey bottles under the floorboards in one of the upstairs bedrooms in our house, when I had occasion to renovate it. I presume left there by a previous tenant. Stephen Coughlan's public house had many tenants, but the previous owner before Stephen Coughlan had it was a Mrs. Bowles. Her name was printed on the bottle labels as the person that bottled it, and the address was 42 St Joseph St. the present address. So it wasn't uncommon for the older generation to think that the bottles on display were other than the real thing.

Several guys worked as barmen from time to time, either for Stephen Coughlan or the others that leased it from him from time to time. Stephen Coughlan had quite a few things going for him in those days. Not alone was he a publican he also had a bookmakers licence to run a book in the local dog track in the Markets Field, and all the dog and horse racing meetings all over the country. That led to him opening a few bookie shops in Limerick City. On top of that he was an active politician and City Councillor, was elected Mayor of Limerick and was also elected a Labour T.D. to Dail Eireann.

Stephen Coughlan had so much going for him, it's no wonder I never remember him serving a pint inside the counter of his own bar. Even though he lived overhead the public house with his wife Peggy and his daughters and two sons Stephen and Thady, by the way his son (Thady was the youngest man ever to be elected Mayor of Limerick years afterwards). The only time I used to see Stephen Coughlan was when he would bring a crowd of his friends to his public house in the early hours of the morning, after coming from a race meeting somewhere around the country.

I could write a book about Stephen Coughlan and his life growing up in Limerick City. Stephen Coughlan was born under the shadow of St Johns Cathedral tower in Gerald Griffin St. and went to school with my father. Many were the drink I enjoyed with him in the bar he once owned but was now taken over by Eric Lynch.

Listening to him telling tales when he was making his way up in the world, it was fascinating stuff to listen to. Charlie Malone's, or W.J.Souths bars were only a few of the bars that Stephen Coughlan, and his old pals like Paddy Kelly, another (ex former Mayor of Limerick), and his close friend Gerry Lillis loved to frequent before he died.

Charlie Malone was one man that had it rented from Stephen Coughlan for a while, before he got a bar of his own in Wolfe Tone St. I mention Charlie Malone in detail in the previous chapter. I remember Charlie saying once he would sell fifteen to twenty timber kegs of Guinness per week. Sure enough each week Charlie had the wall outside in Emmett Place lined up with empty Guinness barrels.

My memories of this pub vary from time to time. As I immigrated to London in 1953 and lived there for seventeen years, until I returned home to live in Limerick for good in 1970. My visits to this pub were on and off every time I returned home on occasional holidays. To get to the gents toilet you had to cross the hall at the end of the bar, that led to the side door of the pub in Emmett Place.

The wall that was used as the urinal divided a big shed that was later used as a boxing club that Stephen Coughlan set up for the local boys in St. Josephs Parish. Many good boxers came out of that boxing club since it was first set up. Vises Field just around the corner from the pub produced some very fine boxers. One of those boxers was a guy called Brendan Murphy.

Brendan lived in Vises Field and was raised with a family called Hen, he was known as Brendan Hen. He was the champion boxer in the Royal Ulster Rifles, and served with me in Cyprus in 1959 when I was doing two years National Service with the British Army.

Stephen Coughlan's big shed was put to use for several operations. I remember an old bathtub that was at the other side of the urinal wall in the public house was used for washing empty stout bottles and getting the old stout labels off for rebottling.

I had good reason to remember the old bathtub, for one reason it was always filled with cold water, weather there were bottles steeping in it or not. I was in the bar one Sunday night after hours and the Civic Guards raided it. We all ran for the toilet to get out over the wall into the shed. I managed to scale the wall and dropped down into the bath of freezing cold water. Everything was pitch black and everyone that came out that way got drenched up to the knees.

I remember another time getting a closer look at that bathtub watching Eric Lynch, another man that worked for Stephen Coughlan, bottling stout and storing them in racks to season before they were sold. Eric Lynch later acquired this from Stephen Coughlan and ran it for nearly forty years.

To give another mention to this famous shed attached to the public house, and was converted at a later date into Eric Lynch's lounge bar. The now famous Tony O'Mara the multimillionaire, he at one time used it. In actual fact he started out doing a bit of panel beating in this shed. He worked in this premises in 1958, I know this for sure, because I engaged one of the men that worked for him, to drive my wife and newborn son out to Abbeyfeale in the Month of November, before I returned to the Army after getting some compassionate leave.

The oldest man I can ever remember drinking in Stephen Coughlan's pub was a man called Dandy Sheehan. He lived straight across from the front door of the pub in number four St. Joseph St.

Dandy used to wear a black bowler hat, and the shirt collars were starched so hard that they appeared to cut into his neck under his chin. The front and back studs of his collar he never seemed to hide then with his black tie. The rest of his dress stuck out like a sore thumb to me also. The only other man he reminded me of was from a photograph of my own grandfather, and he died the year I was born in 1937.

Dandy wore a black waistcoat and had a watch and chain that was fastened to the lapel of his coat; the chain was looped through one buttonhole in his waistcoat and he had the watch in one of the pockets, he kept looking at his watch every few minutes. Dandy used to sit on one of the rows of seats that came out of the Coliseum Cinema in O'Connell St. They were very comfortable upholstered seats, and they had upholstered hand rests also.

They were sort of automatic seats, the kind that every time you stood up the seat would flick up automatically behind you. If I'm not mistaken there were about six seats fixed together in one row. I remember remarking that it was nice to see a souvenir out of one of our favourite cinemas to sit on in one of our local public houses.

The pub was transformed completely when Eric Lynch took it over. The snug went and everything else that I liked about the old bar. The new set-up took in the yard and the shed, and the inside space was such that the bar was divided into two drinking areas, one was a public bar the other became a lounge bar. It also provided Eric and His wife Florence Casey and their family with a larger up stairs living accommodation area.

Eric Lynches wife Florence was an accomplished pianist and organist, the music that she played attracted packed crowds several nights a week. The talented singers both male and female came on a regular basis to show what they could do. They at one stage organised an annual get together that met for a dinner and dance in the Shannon Arms Hotel. They called themselves the Woodpecker Club; I think that the fact that most of the women drank cider had a lot to do with it. This new breed of singers used the assistance of a microphone that had loud speakers.

It often crossed my mind, what would the singers of long ago have thought about it. I knew a few beautiful singers that didn't need a microphone to be heard, Paddy O'Donnell was one of the most popular and favourite ones, he lived to use the new set-up but I often thought he sounded better the old way. Songs and recitations seemed to have a different sound, and people seemed to listen to what was said and sung with more interest.

All those old timers have since passed on, and all we have is the memories they left us. I remember all the old boys and the favourite places in the pub where the used to sit. Guys like Abb Sheehan Frank McCourt's uncle who lived in Little Barrington St. Frank McCourt's mother and grandmother lived in the same lane. If the truth were known most of the people that lived in all the lanes nearby including School House Lane, and the lane known as Little Barrington St. would have used Eric's bar at that time. That of course would have had to include Frank McCourt's father Malachey and his mother Angela, and possibly his grandmother Margaret Sheehan. I know for sure Abb drank there, because I drank with him, up to the time he died around 1972.

The guys I will never forget who drank in our local pub on the corner of Emmett Place, are Kevin known as (Shocker) Farrell, Mick Cowel, Alfie Sheehan, Dandy's Sheehan's son, and great friend of Stephen Coughlan, Danny Sherlock, Paddy O'Donnell, Charlie Macken, Alic Bogue and my own father Christy O'Donovan to name but a very small few. The sons and daughters of those I have mentioned, and many more too numerous to mention are still frequenting this famous old public house at the back of the Monument to the present day.

So much for the public house on the corner of Emmett Place, in St. Joseph St. Where all the residents in the surrounding lanes and streets, used to congregated and render beautiful songs on bonfire nights, after being slung out of our local public house. From the storytellers, singers, dart and ring players, card players and pool players in my opinion their likes will never be seen again.

One final word since Eddie Fraher and Gerry Heddigan took over the lease of Eric's Bar in St. Joseph Street they run it as a no nonsense pub. They have a strong involvement with Thomond Rugby Club. They cater for both regulars and students alike, who frequent this hostelry for light snacks and lunches at very reasonable prices.

Chapter 27
W. J. South's Bar

W J South's public house is located in Quinlan St, about one hundred yards away from the Daniel O'Connell Monument also known locally as the Crescent, Quinlan St, is the smallest St, in Limerick City it has only six houses. My first memory of ever going into Willie South's bar was with my father and the year was 1951. The reason I remember that particular date is, it's the year my father moved into our new house in Emmett Place. The Month was May I know because there were two Lilac trees growing in the garden at the back of our house, and Lilac trees are only in bloom for one Month in May, and they were in full bloom.

The reason I was taken to South's public house was to celebrate a house warming party with my uncles and aunts. My uncle Tony had recently moved into a house he bought in 20, Barrington St. just around the corner from South's bar. That was another reason for the double house warming celebration. It was a great feeling to be made a fuss of, even if it was only for one day and to celebrate with all my first cousins.

Looking at the front entrance of South's as it is today it only slightly resembles the old front as I remembered it. Of course the name hasn't changed over the door. But there were two door entrances and a large window in the middle displaying tins of biscuits, boxes of chocolate, and a huge selection of spirits from wines to every brand of drink on the market. I always admired the window display especially at Christmas time, the holly and ivy the coloured lights and paper decorations, he always had huge assortment of boxes of Christmas crackers.

When you entered the door on the left of the front window it led into an off licence shop measuring about sixteen foot square. This off licence shop did a roaring trade not alone from the passing custom on the street, but by clients that frequented the bar to have a leisurely drink. Centre ways inside the counter in the off licence, was a small door that gave Willie South or members of his staff access to move from inside the public bar, to and from the off licence shop. There was a hatch cut into this small door for passing small items of goods in or out from either the off licence or the bar, for large orders the door would be opened, but was always kept closed for privacy.

When you pushed open the door on the right hand side to enter South's public house, it led into a hallway that led into the bar, this hall separated the off licence from the pub. The first thing that caught my eye was the black and white three-inch square tiles on the hallway floor. They were set out in a kind of diamond shape in the middle that finished in a square border about nine inches all around. As soon as the second door leading into the front part of the bar was opened. The floor tiles changed colour to a terracotta brown. The tile floor stopped about eight feet away from the hall door. From there on right through the bar, until you came to the lane at the back door, the floors were just bare timber floorboard.

The counter in South's bar started where the off licence hatch was. I always thought the counter looked very high. I know Willie South wasn't very tall, but even to sit on one of the very many bar stools, I always had to reach up for the drink. The first drink I can ever remember drinking in South's bar was a large bottle of O'Sullivan's orangeade. There were two sizes of mineral bottles but I got the large one. I can still get the sensation of the fizz going up my nose after I gulped a mouthful down after drinking it out of the bottle, it also made me cough and sneeze to the delight of my cousins.

Looking up at the high wooden wainscoted walls and ceiling and gazing over the bar counter was a fascinating sight to see. The first thing I noticed was the six beautiful bevelled mirrors encased in a timber frame mantle, I would have thought made especially to house the mirrors, and to show them off to best effect. This frame was coated with many coats of black lacquer that made the whole piece glitter as if it had been highly varnished.

The mirrors alone were a talking point, just for the workmanship that must have went into them, and the stories that went with them. I remember my father telling me the story behind some of those mirrors. There is a circle of dots set out on those mirrors that represented the four provinces in Ireland. If you can imagine looking at a clock, but instead of twelve numbers there is thirty-two dots, now think of a compass pointing North, put a dot there in brackets like so (O). Then go down South and put a dot there in brackets, do the very same with East and West. Then fill in eight dots in each quarter all around. The picture you should get is a circle with thirty-six dots, North, South, East, and West, are in brackets.

The story goes the dots in brackets represent each one of the four provinces of Ireland, which are, Ulster, Munster, Leinster, and Connaught. The dots in between represent the thirty-two counties in those provinces. Making the total amount of counties thirty-two. That would have been when Ireland was united even though it was under British Rule.

The engravings on the mirrors may tell a different story for other people, from different parts of Ireland. As regards the Limerick connection there is an engraving of the treaty stone, to signify why Limerick is known as the city of the broken treaty. It depends on how each person interprets them, either way they are a nice sight to see. There were other beautiful framed tapestries fixed on different walls in different areas of South's bar. I remember several Americans would have paid a small fortune to buy Willie South's mirrors, or the framed tapestries if he would sell them. I'm glad to say that they are still in the bar to this day.

Over the years I have had several chances to observe Willie South and his staff in action in the every day running of his public house. Before ever the iron lung was invented in the days when Guinness came in timber barrels. Willie South had a small contraption that was made for him by one of his carpenter customers. When the biggest barrel was rolled from the road into the bar. This contraption was used to manoeuvre the barrel through an opening in the counter until it was capsized into its final position for pulling pints.

The next job was to tap it ready to start filling porter. I observed the way he used to tap the barrels. He would take a brass tap especially used for drawing Guinness from a barrel. The tap was then wrapped in a towel ready to stop any spatters when the tap was driven into the bung provided at the bottom of the barrel. A clear warning was given before Willie or any of his barmen attempted to drive the tap into the barrel. They would give everyone in the bar plenty of time to move away or to duck down. Then with a mighty blow the mallet would drive the tap home, much to everyone's delight. Sometimes it might take two or three belts of the mallet to achieve this. I have witness spatters hitting the ceiling with the pressure in some of those barrels, bearing in mind the ceiling is up to twelve feet high in South's bar.

The pressure in the barrel could be adjusted by drilling a small hole in the barrel with a carpenters bit and brace, then closing it off by tapping a small wooden bung into it. I often remember coming into the bar after the confraternity was over on Monday nights. There was often two lines of started pints of Guinness running the whole length of the bar counters, over sixty pints or more, all ready to be topped off as the men came in and called for them.

Willie South always had an excellent bar staff each one wearing a long brown overall coat. Another memory that crosses my mind, Willie South never allowed women into his public house. He did all in his power to discourage them from coming in. The first thing he would say is, he didn't have a ladies room, the only toilet in the pub was for gents.

But for some unknown reason there was one woman he used to serve. She was an old woman that wore a black shawl by the name of Annie Tracy. She always sat at the edge of the seat inside the front door. Annie Tracy used to drink one or two half-pints of Guinness every day then go home. She lived in Vises Court off Saint Joseph St. and I was told that she was one of the last members of the famous Tracy family from the Parish, which sold Packet and Tripe all over Limerick City. Her family name was more famous in Limerick City in those days for Packet and Tripe than the Irish Republican Army and I mean that. The packet and tripe Tracy family, is still talked about in Limerick to this present day.

The changes I have seen, and remembering the old characters I have known since Willie South decided to retire and throw the towel in. It has inspired me to write about other experiences I have had in a variety of public houses in Limerick City.

David Hickey is the new proprietor of South's bar, and has been since his family purchased it in 1972. He decided to make a few changes for the better to improve the bar to bring it up to date. The first thing he sorted out was the problem with the toilets. I ought mention at this stage that when Dave Hickey and his dear wife Peg took over South's bar they were fortunate to have Willie South stay on for a few Months to keep an eye on things to help them settle in.

It was great to see his old familiar face inside the bar, this time as an employee. I couldn't help noticing how he would take to women coming into the public house, after the new ladies and gents toilets were installed. Willie South was a bachelor and his only hobby was investing in stocks and shares, and collecting miniature replicas of toy trains, he loved train spotting. In my opinion he certainly had no time for women.

But women's Lib changed all that, the more renovations that were carried out in South's bar, the more women that started to frequent it, and he was around to witness what must have been for him the biggest change in his lifetime. Willie South died a few short years after he sold his legendary public house. It's a pity he didn't live to witness the fame South's bar got, as a result of a book written by Frank McCourt.

Frank McCourt told a few fibs about South's bar that I know for a fact were not true. The only reason he mentioned South's bar was the fact it was across the road from Saint Josephs Church and around the corner from where he lived with his grandmother. And the name over South's door hadn't changed since he remembered it as a child. The Parish clerk of Saint Josephs Church Steven Carey that he mentions in his book is in the sketch in the snug in South's bar.

From Willie South's time I'm bringing the South's bar story on another few decades to the present day. I have witnessed a few more funny experiences like the Sunday I was in the bar drinking with my old pals. It was a year or two after 1978 the year Munster beat the New Zealand all Blacks, in Thomond Park here in our own Limerick City. Dave Hickey got a large framed picture of some of the action of the historic victory over the New Zealand team; this was hung up on the wall in South's Bar.

In those days we were left drinking up to about 3pm before the barman closed up until it was time to open up again at 5pm. I remember going to the toilet and I thought I was the last man left. Tom O'Connor the head barman made a rough check and we left the bar together. It transpired that one of our friends Paddy McNamara the coalman. (I will have more to say about this man in another chapter), was locked in the bar.

To hear Paddy tell of his experiences was priceless. His first thought was to sample some of the tempting top shelf optics. He taught about using the phone but didn't know whose number to phone. He wanted to get word to his wife but they had no phone. He was afraid to move around too much in case the burglar alarm went off.
So he decided to sit looking at the picture on the wall and studying all the names of the two teams the day Munster beat the all Blacks.

You can imagine the fright Dave Hickey got when he came in and found Paddy McNamara waiting to be left out. If ever you had a question about the names of the guys that played that rugby match on that December day in Thomond Park, when Munster won by nine points to nil against the New Zealand all blacks. Paddy McNamara was your man. He used to tell me he studied every little detail in that photograph, until it was etched in his mind for all time; by the way this photograph is still hanging on the wall somewhere in South's bar.

The names of the guys I knew and loved so much unfortunately most of them are gone to their eternal rest. There is a framed sketch in the front snug, that they now call the Senate. The original Senate is positioned middle ways in the public house. Most of the guys in that sketch were regular drinkers in South's bar, but would have isolated themselves in this little hideaway in the old Senate.

The real genuine characters were to be found at the back of the bar, where the kitchen is now. If a sketch were to be commissioned around that time, of the guys that frequented that area of the bar, or any area outside the Senate, it would fill every inch of the walls. My very close friends like Paddy Bourke and his nephew John Lyons, Denis Doyle, Jack Hayes, Hugh Nolan, Paddy and Gerry O'Halloran, Paddy McNamara, Jimmy Gubbin's, Mick Byrne's, Bill Bindy, Johnny Whelan, Eddie Deignum, Gerry Leddin, and my own father to name but a very few. There was never a dull moment if you happened to be in anyone of those guys company.

I could fill ten A 4 pages if I had to name every one of the guys I had the pleasure of being in their company with at one time or another. Unfortunately most of them are no longer with us, but I always remember them in my prayers. Just to give you a good example of the wit of some of those men.

I remember one story that used to be repeated over and over about the demon drink and the mere garden worm. This story was brought into the pub by one of the regular Monday night guys that attended the Holy Family Confraternity. The Mission Priest giving the sermon from the pulpit the highest point in the Church. Chose the subject of (Demon Drink) and what it can do to the insides of a person's body.

To demonstrate this he had a glass of whiskey in one hand, and a common garden earthworm in the other. He dropped the worm into the whiskey and held the glass as high as he could, asking everyone in the Church to look at it. The poor worm wriggled and wriggled until it dropped to the bottom of the glass, presumably stone dead.

"Look at that my dear brethren he said, if whiskey will do that to a humble earth worm what must it do to your bodies"? He went on then about homes and marriages being broken up over the demon drink. Finally when the sermon was over and all the men had left the Church. The bell rang in the sacristy door, and the Missionary Priest answered it. There was a man standing there that wanted to talk to him.

When the Priest asked your man what he wanted, poor man said he was very impressed with the sermon and wanted to know if the Priest could give him the price of a glass of whiskey. "What for the Priest asked?" poor man said, "Because I think I'm full of worms Father".

Before I conclude this chapter I must pay tribute to Dave and Peg Hickey, and I'm sure the rest of his family members for the magnificent alterations they have had carried out to W J South's public house. The designer responsible for the new look South's is Adrienne Florance Purcell. She excelled herself with her plans to give this famous old pub a push into the twenty first century. The original piece of furniture housing the six bevelled mirrors behind the main bar counter were the inspiration for Adrienne to give W J south's it's new look.

The design copied from some of the original old bevelled mirrors that were first installed in 1909. This centrepiece behind the main bar has been given a new lease of life with touches of 22-carrot gold leaf skilfully placed by young Randal Hotkinson. Again the designer excelled herself with her choice of lighting fixtures and surrounding acoustics.

The sand blasted glass made in Ireland and designed by Adrienne herself, she told me, "The whole idea of the pub was opulence at it's best and there was a lot of Italian Irish influence in her design". She went on to say that, "Irish crafts men went to Italy to cut the marble twenty-two mils thick. This marble was used for the floors". Adrienne had so much to tell me about her design unfortunately I'm limited to the text in this chapter.

Finally credit equally has to go to the perfectionists namely to all the trades involved in the great job that was carried out in my old public house. It gladdens my heart to know we have such qualified talented craftsmen in Ireland to carry out such a task.

W J South's is worth a visit just to see the beautiful work that has been carried out on it from top to bottom. It's a good feeling to know that my old public house is up there with the best of the rest, and in my estimation I would go as far as to say it is the best. The Author of "Angela's ashes" will be pleasantly surprised with some of the changes and I'm sure when you visit it you will agree?

Chapter 28
The Windmill Bar

The Windmill Bar is in Upper Henry Street, and was beside the house where the famed (Sean South from Garryowen) was born. I frequented this pub on and off for about three years when I returned home from England with my wife and four children in August 1970. I had lost my only daughter in a road accident in London in April 1967. I wasn't sad to see the back of London after earning my living over there for the previous seventeen years.

My father frequented this pub also, and he introduced me to the owner at the time Jimmy Condon. Jimmy originally came from Castle Connell. When Jimmy found out I was a carpenter he asked me to do a job of work in his public house. He had purchased a huge bar counter in Fitzes Auction yard up rear end of the New Street and Ballinacurra. This counter originally came out of a pub called the Old Stand on the corner of Clontarf Place and Henry Street.

Jimmy Condon asked me if I could do the job at night in order to keep his place open during the day. Most of his customers worked in the cement factory and around the dockland area. I agreed and said I would do whatever I could during the day and keep the night work for when the pub would have to be closed. I had plenty of room to set up a bench to work on outside as he had a huge back yard. Most of the cutting I had to do was outside so I didn't interfere with the guzzlers drinking porter inside.

When it came to move the counter after I had finished with it outside into the bar that job was left for the night. Needless to say I had plenty of able bodies only too willing to help, especially with the promise of a free jar or two. I always managed to have an audience, to see what the guy from London could do. After all he was Christy O'Donovan's son and no one had heard of any carpenters in the O'Donovan family the were all tailors.

I had put up a thirteen foot long studded partition inside the counter, it went from floor to ceiling about nine foot high. This partition divided the front door and formed the hallway giving privacy and dividing the bar from the rest of the house. There were two door openings one that let to the stairs and basement down below. The other gave access to the hall and led to the upstairs part of the house. Both sides of the partition I covered with sheets of chipboard. The doorframes were fixed and doors hung and completely finished off locks architrave and all. The old snug I dismantled and re-used the Piranha Pine to use elsewhere in the bar.

The last job I left for to do at night was to stick the full sheets of Formica to the bar side of the studded partition, before the counter could be lifted into place. Jimmy decided that mirrors were too troublesome to clean. He chose an imitation teak pattern that was in keeping with the highly varnished piranha pine sheeting. I decided to come in around twelve midnight to do the Formica. I had cut all the sheets and dry fitted them in the day, in the order I wanted them to go up on the wall, and was ready to stick them that night.

I knocked to be left in to the bar around half an hour after midnight, thinking the place would be empty. To my surprise I had an audience of about eight guys waiting to see how I was going to stick eight foot by four sheets of Formica inside the counter to the partition wall that I had got ready some days previously. I might add they seemed to me to be all inebriated, including Jimmy Condon.

I cleared all the tables and stools away to one side of the bar room, in the hope they would take the hint and move off home. No such luck they wanted to see something before they went home.

I set up a simple workbench in the middle of the floor just two-carpenter stools, and two sheets of eight by four three-quarter plywood. This was the perfect height for me for the work I had to do. The back door was wide open that is where I set up the bench. It is important to have as much ventilation when using evo-stick glue. The first sheet of Formica to go up was two-foot six wide by eight foot high. I knew when I opened the gallon can of evo-stick and began to apply it to the Partition the strong smell would certainly drive some of my audience away.

Sure enough the coughing started and then one guy said, "Jesus let me out of here". All I could do was laugh; it takes a good constitution to put up with the smell of evo-stick glue. I was well used to it as I had done countless similar jobs in banks and bars in London. I actually liked the smell of it. As I said it is important to have good ventilation, otherwise you could get a headache.

The boys scattered and took their pints out side into the yard. I warned them to keep out of my way or to go home. I had a long night ahead of me and needed to give the job in hand my full attention. I was beginning to loose my cool as Jimmy kept coming inside the counter to fill more drinks as he was half pissed himself. They eventually drifted off in dribs and drabs out the back gate. Jimmy's wife took him up to bed and at last I was alone. I persevered through the night and finished about five o'clock in the morning.

The first knock at the pub window in the morning brought Jimmy's wife down. She said that would be some of her Cement factory customers looking for a drink to help them sleep after coming off night work. As it happened they were two Kerry men and they were in digs next door to the pub. They were the first to congratulate me for the work I done during the night. If I may say so myself they were very impressed. I joined them in a drink on the house from Jimmy's wife.

Before I went home for a few hours sleep, I made arrangements for Jimmy to contact a plumber some time that morning to disconnect the water from the sink in the old counter, and to connect up the glass washer and water to the sink in the new counter when it was lifted in. All the revalent breweries had to be there also to run their beer taps to the new counter. I knew this job for my part wouldn't take long just a straight swap over I had everything ready just to lift it into position. I managed to be back on the job around 11o'clock that morning after a few hours sleep and a good breakfast; I was ready for the final part of the operation.

When it came to move the counter into the bar, after I had finished most of the alteration work on it outside in the yard. I had spent several hours days before hand, cutting an access hatch and door opening in the counter, making sure that there wouldn't be much more to do on it after it was lifted into place. Needless to say I had plenty of able bodies only too willing to help, especially with the promise of a free jar or two. A small man from Watergate was the plumber he went by the nickname of "Ballcock". He was an excellent plumber and we worked well together.

The counter was lifted into position at eleven o'clock in the morning and myself and Ballcock and the others tradesmen involved got to work. By the way it took eight strong men to lift in the counter into position. The helpers got "Danos" or pint bottles of Guinness, for their help. The draught Beers and Guinness were flowing from the taps in the new counter less than two hours afterwards; needless to say a cheer went for the workforce.

Apart from a few pelmets to conceal the fluorescent lighting, and replacing and repositioning the bottle storage shelving to suit the new set-up, there was very little more for me to do. Admittedly I had quite a bit of making and matching up outside the counter to do as regards the seating where it had been disturbed to accommodate the new counter. All in all I was well pleased the way things worked out, and knowing the way the grapevine worked in Limerick at that time. I knew that one job would lead to another eventually, when the word got round.

Jimmy Condon let the word out that he was throwing a bit of a get together for his regulars to celebrate the new look to his establishment the following weekend. Naturally I attended with my father and my wife Noreen we were invited to meet some of his closest friends. Very few of them knew me as I had been away in London for nearly seventeen years.

Little did we know the treat that was laid on for us that night? Apart from the drink being on the house, there were beautiful sandwiches and finger-licking food handed around in abundance. Then as the crack began to liven up a man was introduced as the Master of Ceremony's or M.C. for short. He called everyone to order and said, "There were quite a good few well-known talented singers in the bar. He went on to say that the only voices he wished to hear, was his own and the person he would ask to sing".

Everyone said, "here, here". He then proceeded to call my own father as the first singer. I overheard my father say to his mates I'm not ready yet; I have had only two pints. The M.C. said, " For the benefit of those of you who don't know the beautiful renovations to Jimmy Condon's Bar was carried out by Christy O'Donovan's son Austin who is here tonight with his lovely wife Noreen". He went on to say, "That we recently came home from London, then wished us and our young family well, and hoped we would settle in Limerick for good.

Everyone cheered and clapped us, then called for Christy O'Donovan to sing. The M.C. called, "Order please, order, one voice one singer". Dad started to sweat and gave a rendition of one of his favourite songs. The Last Rose Of Summer followed by; Thee Old Refrain was the songs he chose to sing. I never heard him sing so well, I was really proud of him. The hairs at the back of my head stood out with sheer delight and pride. I knew whoever followed him it would be a hard act to follow.

Everyone who was called on to sing after my father was better than the next. Paddy O'Donnell otherwise known as Paddy "O" sang, "Danny Boy, and Myra My Girl". The people that couldn't sing some said over twenty verse recitations. From "Dangerous Dan McGrew, to the Charge of the Light Brigade". As the night was beginning come to a close, the M.C. was constantly being called on to call Christy O'Donovan's son up to sing.

Suddenly I could not believe my ears when I heard my name being called out to sing. I was petrified and didn't know where to turn, all my protest not to sing seemed to fall on deaf ears. Then I heard my father saying to my wife Noreen, "Can he sing". With that she nudged me to sing. With that I stood up to say that an American named Hoagy Carmichael wrote the only song I ever learned the words of. I went on to say that to my knowledge it had never been recorded. I then started to sing it went something like this.

I should have known you years ago, where on earth were you, long years ago,
We missed so much and dreamed, so little, before you set, my heart aglow.
You should have seen, the way you smiled, as we travelled each, long lonely mile,
But we-el go, on, from here together, as if I'd known you, all the while.

I am even jealous, of the flowers in spring, they knew, long ago, about you,
They heard the laughter, and the songs you sang, through all the years, I spent, without you. I wish that I could truly say, that I knew you, long, before today,
But we-el go on, from here together, as if I'd known you all the while.
(Repeat)
I am even jealous, of the flowers in spring, they knew, long ago, about you,
They heard the laughter, and the songs you sang, through all the years, I spent, without you. I wish that I could truly say, that I knew you, long, before today,
But we-el go on, from here together, as if I'd known you all the while.

When I finished I saw tears running down my fathers face, it would have been his first time ever hearing me singing, and the words of that beautiful song were very appropriate for the get together we were having in Jimmy Condon's public house that night. The M.C. had the last say and to round it off with his usual party piece.

After much shouting for him to sing he started to fold two sheets of newspaper and then started tearing then into strips, concealing as much of what he was doing at the same time, while telling us that the song he was about to sing was made famous by a favourite singer of his called Arthur Tracy. He then told us the title of the song was, "Trees", it went something like this.

"I think that I shall never see, a poem lovely as a tree.
A tree whose hungry mouth is prayer, against the earth deep blowing breath, a tree's as looks as though those old days, and lifts her leafy arms to pray.

A tree that May in summer wear, a nest of robins in her hair,
Upon whose bosoms no have claim, who with their medleys sips with rain. Oh with our name while fools like me, but only God can make a tree".

It's the way he went about it, and his actions as he sang it, one couldn't help but admire this man he eventually finished on his knee unfolding the paper up and up until it reached the ceiling, the final words of his song being, " Only God can make a tree". It was one of the best nights free entertainment my wife Noreen and I had since we returned home to live in Limerick City.

Chapter 29
Willie Sextons

Willie Sexton's public house is almost straight across from the Windmill Bar in Henry St. It is one of many public houses in Limerick city that was bought by an ex rugby player. Willie sexton was one of those very good Garryowen rugby players. My nephew Don (Gooner) O'Donovan an ex Garryowen hooker never fails to visit Willies pub when he is in town, he likes to meet his old buddies from his rugby days, Willie Sexton's is that place.

I knew it as Joe (The Phantom) O'Brien's Bar. To my knowledge Joe O'Brien had two brothers, one was called Tom, he worked inside the bar with Joe. The other I only knew by his nickname, they used to call him (Pizzy). Pizzy was a bookie's runner and used to clerk for some bookie up in Wolfe Tone St. To my knowledge Pizzy wouldn't be seen dead inside a bar counter filling pints. Joe O'Brien's nickname was the Phantom; he got that from wandering around the streets late at night well after closing time.

I always thought that name suited him down to the ground. Joe had a very sallow complexion, more like a Greek than an Irishman, everything about Joe looked sinister. He was the nearest thing to the film star Boris Karloff I ever saw. His black hair and bushy eyebrows, and his jet black eyes used to glint when he looked at you. You would get the impression he could look straight into your soul. Having said that Joe was a very kind-hearted man. He would help out anyone if he thought they were in trouble. I know this from what friends of mine told me.

Most of the Phantom's customers worked in the Dockland area and lived in the Windmill and O'Curry St. area. A fare share of his customers worked in the Gas Works. In those days the Town Gas as it was called was extracted from coal. Coal boats arrived in Limerick like a shuttle service between keeping the Gas Works and the coal yards supplied. It was non-stop winter and summer, as I remember it.

Joe O'Brien's public house was one long bar with the counter running down on the right hand side as you entered it. The seating ran the whole length of the bar in the shape of furms more like the seating one would find in St Joseph's Church without the hand-rest. There was a deep shelf behind the seating to rest the drinks on. Two narrow partition divisions broke up the counter and there were high stools between those divisions all in all about twenty people would fill the front bar area.

A room at the end of the bar and at the back of the pub measuring about sixteen feet by twelve feet was where the radio was. There were sufficient tables and chairs in this room for about ten more people. Most of Joe O'Brien's customers that wanted to stay on after hours on Sundays, used to make for the back room. Needless to say Joe would call time up, if there were any guys in that room that he thought or was told that could be troublesome. He would clear the whole house and let his customers know the secret knock to get in later on, after the troublemakers took off.

I had occasion on one particular Sunday to be caught in that back room with a few of my friends. They were all waiting for Michael O'Hehir to give the commentary of the Munster final between Tipperary and Limerick. From what I remember about that match the referee blew up ten minutes before full time, and there was almost a riot in the stadium. Michael O'Hehir was doing his nut, and said he thought the referee had gone crazy, everyone was roaring and shouting at the ref, but to no avail.

Both teams were level scores and they all walked off the pitch together. An announcement was later made saying that the game would have to be played two weeks from that date in the same venue. Needless to say that was the talking point for the remainder of that day in all the public houses and elsewhere. For my part I was just glad to be left out of Joe O'Brien's to go home and eat a bit of dinner. I wasn't a hardened drinker like some of my mates, but I enjoyed the excitement and trill of being in a public house after hours. It gave me a sort of manly feeling and I liked the experience.

One regular in the Phantoms pub at the time was Paddy McNamara, I mention him in chapter twelve of this book. Paddy worked for Ted Castles coal merchants in the Dock Road. He used to deliver coal in Limerick City when he drove a horse and cart. When the horse died Paddy graduated to driving a small petrol driven lorry. His territory was extended to the counties Clare, Tipperary, and the borders of Kerry.

Paddy's horse and cart was a dead giveaway to know where to find him in a public house. The horse was given a nosebag with oats to eat and a bucket of water to drink. When the horse was seen to, then it was Paddy's turn to sample a couple of pints of Diesel meaning Guinness to wash the coal dust down as he used to call it.

Without doubt Paddy McNamara was the strongest man in his hay day I ever saw, he was over six foot tall and worked very hard.

He told me he carried heavy bag of coal up three of four flights of stairs, to elderly people living in the high houses in O'Connell St and the tenement houses in Arthur's Quay. Sometimes two or three trips were necessary to deliver the order. The bags used to hold up to ten stone of coal each.

Paddy McNamara lived in Spelicy Square off Wolfe Tone St. with his mother. When she died Paddy started dating a lovely woman from Moyasta near Kilkee in County Clare. Both of them were mature when they got married, and were very happy in each other's company. He told me they loved to do a bet on the horses on Saturdays and play cards at night at home.

His wife worked selling tickets in the City Theatre in Sexton St. facing the Christian Brothers School. She was also very good with figures and dabbled in a bit of accountancy, doing the books for her employer, who also had a hotel in Thomas St. Paddy often showed me a racing docket that she would have written out, showing the beautiful handwriting she had written. Paddy was always good for a few free passes either for the cinema or the occasional stage shows that were put on from time to time.

Two of Paddy McNamara's favourite songs were "On top of old Smokey" and "Frankie and Johnny were lovers". As soon as you walked into any pub that Paddy was in, if he sang a song it was always one of those two. He had an awful habit of starting a song and bursting out laughing after the first line of the song. He done that after every line of the song, no matter what happened.

I remember my father giving out to him saying, "For Christ sake finish the song and do your laughing after." No good the more he was checked it made him laugh louder. He would have the whole public house laughing before he was finished. Paddy was just one howl of laughter. You would hear guys saying when Paddy was asked to sing,

"Oh Jesus spare us from Paddy Mack's laugh". That was enough to start him off before he started to sing.

Paddy had loads of jokes; I suppose that's why he kept laughing all the time. He used to get himself into such a state from laughing; I think he just got flashbacks of jokes that came into his mind from time to time. One good one he told about two brothers he met in a pub in Clare, when he was delivering coal down there. It seems the brothers used to drink together, and Paddy asked them if they were farmers, one of them answered, "Not anymore sir. He then said to his brother, "Open your mouth John and show the nice man where our farm went, along with twenty thousand pounds".

Another famous one he told was about the woman he met in town, which wanted him to deliver a half a ton of coal to her house. Ted Castles had reduced the size of the bags of coal from ten stone bags to eight stone bags. That made Paddy Mack's job somewhat easier. It just meant he had to make more trips in and out of houses to deliver his loads. Eight stone equalled one hundredweight, twenty hundred weights equalled a ton, for Paddy to deliver a half a ton he had to bring ten eight stone bags of coal to her house.

Now getting back to the woman, she said she would leave the money on the mantle-piece over the fireplace. She told him he could get the key of the front door under the flowerpot on the right hand side of the garden path on his way into the passage. Paddy said, " Ok he would deliver it sometime in the afternoon". The story goes when he delivered the coal and went to look for the money. He couldn't find it on the mantle-piece. Then a voice cried out," Look under the clock mister, it's under the clock Sir".

Paddy was shocked, and tried to find out where the strange voice was coming from, then he realised the voice was coming from the cage in the corner of the room; it was the woman's pet parrot talking. Paddy scratched his said and spoke out loud to himself, saying, "Jesus I never knew a parrot could talk as good as that". The words were no sooner out of his mouth when the parrot spoke again saying, "Bring in another bag of coal mister, I can count as well".

Another character I must mention is Tom Hannon, he was called Blackie he lived with his mother somewhere around the Wind Mill district. Tom worked in McMahon's timber yard in the Dock Road. What I remember about Tom most was his skill with a snooker cue. I often won money by backing Tom in tournaments that would have been organised in the more popular snookers halls like Burtons. In my opinion he could have gone far if he took it up professionally.

Tom was a good-looking guy and was always dressed to kill. He sort of fancied himself as a second Rudolf Valentino. Valentino used to drive the ladies all over the world crazy in those days. When his pictures were shown in the Limerick Cinemas they were sure to draw huge crowds. Tom never failed to have a good-looking bird hanging off his arm and made the most of it.

His black curly hair was always saturated in brilliantine hair oil, and he always managed to wear a wide multicoloured tie with a snow-white shirt, under a well-tailored two-piece Danus Executive suit. I can vouch for those suits because they were made in my uncle's factory in Dominic St. the price was twenty nine pounds ten shillings a go.

Unfortunately when Toms mother died he sort of left himself go, packed up going out with women and relied on Arthur Guinness. From they're on his only priorities was his job, smoking cigarettes, and backing a few horses, and frequenting the local public houses, in that order. He never married but he often told me he never regretted the life he led. In my opinion Tom Hannon could have gone on to be one of the best snooker in Ireland, but it was not to be.

Most people that knew Tom Hannon would have marked him down as a very loveable and quiet spoken man. I just thought he should get a mention from me, as one of the great characters that frequented Joe (The Phantom) O'Brien's public house.

Before I close I would like to finish this chapter on a happier note, by telling you one rather funny joke I heard from one of my best friends Denis Doyle, these were his exact words. "When Neil Armstrong landed on the moon, his famous words were (One small step for man, one giant leap for mankind). He is said to have uttered something else that only NASA could hear, something to the effect of " Good Luck Mr Gorsky".

Years later he was asked to explain what he meant. Apparently, as a little boy, he went into his neighbour's garden to retrieve a baseball. As he bent down to get the ball near the bedroom window, Neil Armstrong heard the neighbour's wife exclaim during an argument, that she would only have sex with her husband when the little boy next door walked on the moon. Thinking of that remark he whispered. Good Luck again Mr Gorsky.

Chapter 30

Kennedy O'Brien's Bar

Kennedy O'Brien's bar is situated in Lower Hartstonege St. just off O'Connell St. I used to frequent this public house on and off to meet my father on occasions. Paddy Hoare owned it he was a local builder in Limerick. He used the upper part of his public house as his office to conduct his building business. I rarely ever drank in it when Paddy Hoare had it. But when he sold it to a Northern Ireland man called Joe Mallon, I started to go in there, Joe Mallon was a Belfast man.

He once told me he had two public houses in Belfast and both of them were blown to smithereens. That's why he got out of Northern Ireland and moved to Limerick to settle. He bought a house in Castletroy and he loved the slow pace of life in Limerick away from the hustle and bustle of Belfast, and the never-ending troubles up there.

Joe Mallon told me a story about two I.R.A. guys that were on the run in the republic of Ireland. It seems roadblocks were set up all over the country looking for them. It happens that the names of the wanted men were Joe and Kevin Mallon. Joe the publican had a son also named Kevin. He was a big lad and attended the University

College Limerick. Joe told me he was driving his son to the school one morning and was stopped, at a checkpoint somewhere on the Dublin road.

The cop that stopped him asked him, "who he was", when he said, "Joe Mallon" the cop said, "Oh yeah and I suppose the guy sitting beside you is Kevin Mallon". Joe said, "Yes it is". Bear in mind Joe Mallon the publican had no identification or driving licence on him and found it very hard time trying to convince the copper who he said he was. To make matters worse Joe Mallon had a very pronounced Belfast accent.

I suppose every time a new governor takes over a public house he will get a certain amount of curiosity customers, especially if he is out of town. I recon that's how my father came to be a customer of Kennedy O'Brien's. Apart from the fact that there was one barman working for the new governor in Kennedy O'Brien's, that had worked in South's for a while, and my father liked to call in to have a chat with him from time to time.

One man that I will never forget used to live in a flat across the street from Kennedy O'Brien's public house. He always dressed in a clean brown overall coat and wore a straw hat. I never saw him dressed in anything else, and I had good reason to know him, he was called Bulleen Ryan. I remember Bulleen Ryan when I lived in Garryowen as a child. He had a huge farm of land he sold it when he retired to the Limerick Corporation.

Most of the Garryowen houses are built on the land that was owed by Bulleen Ryan. He used to chase my friends and me out of his fields, I don't know which was worst, him or the bull in his field, either way they would frighten the shite out of you. I was glad that he never recognised me from the rough times I used to give him as a kid. Bulleen Ryan never married I don't know who got his money he lived alone in Hartstonege St, and is gone to join all the farmers in the sky. He was another character in Kennedy O'Brien's

Joe Mallon for some reason adored my father; he seemed to take to him straight away from the first time they met. My father used to meet his working pals in Kennedy O'Brien's most of them were retired the same as himself. Every Friday morning they would all gather and walk over to the Labour Exchange to collect their stamp money. They would meet another crowd in Paddy Maloney's or the Desmond Arms bars and bring them back to Kennedy O'Brien's to finish their day out drinking.

My father spent forty-eight years working in Cleeve's Condensed Milk Company. When he retired most of the guys he worked with was either retired or about too. They loved meeting up every payday in the Labour Exchange, mind you it was rather embarrassing for two of them in particular, Ignatius Hennihan and Arthur Bourke, they were both bosses in Cleeve's factory. I remember my father telling me they were queuing up in the Labour Exchange one day to get paid, and one guy in the queue, recognised Arthur Bourke.

It seems Arthur Bourke sacked him at one time, and your man let go a string of abuse calling him every rude name under the sun. When Arthur got to the hatch to get paid your man let go again saying, " How does it feel now to be idle and getting handouts you lousy Bastard". All poor Arthur could do was cower away and was glad to get into the pub and soak up a couple of small ones to try and forget that confrontation. But unfortunately he might have had to run that gauntlet the next time he had to go to the Labour Exchange. As my father used to say that thing runs hand in hand when you take on responsibility.

Kennedy O'Brien's public house was really one large big room that had a sort of horseshoe bar. Joe Mallon called the inside part of this pub a lounge bar. The space around the door was supposed to be the public bar. The only sign to signify the difference between the public and the lounge bar was a metal strip screwed to the floor at one corner of the counter.

I often thought Joe Mallon was mean, because if three guys were standing at the bar and a round of drink was called for, he would charge the extra couple of pence, for the guy standing on or over the line on the floor. That friggen line was the cause of a lot of arguments. The men's toilets were in the public bar side of the pub, and guys that came in and went to the toilet first but called for drink on the way in, were charged the low price. When they had paid for their drinks and took them around the corner into the lounge bar side, this was the cause of more rows.

One bar fly in particular that sat at the counter beside the toilets was Joe Mallon's eyes and ears in the pub this guy didn't miss a trick, he was like a house detective for Joe Mallon. He was supposed to be doing a line with the bar maid that came with the pub, in other words she worked for the previous owner Paddy Hoare. I couldn't believe it when my father told me he was going out with this bar maid steady for donkey's years.

They could be seen together at dances and the pictures very often, and he would sit at the bar talking to her every time he came in from work. No sign of asking her to marry him. He kept putting it off and off, until I believe she gave him an ultimatum about getting married. It was no good he wouldn't budge, she dropped him and married another guy who used to sit beside him in Kennedy O'Brien's. The funny thing was they turned out to be the best of friends for years after. I used to see them together in the pub, and quite often in the British Legion Club. The Legion was second next door to Kennedy

O'Brien's public house.

The two boys used to frequent this club to play snooker or billiards, and occasionally go up stairs to the bar for a drink. I happened to be in the Legion one day and had my name down in the book to play a game of snooker. There were two tables in there and it cost sixpence to play for a half hour.

One experience I had of the British Legion Club, which comes to mind, was the day I was in there about 1952. I had my name in the book to play a game of snooker, and I was the next guy to play when one of the two tables were available. Suddenly the door opened a crowd of men came in including the guy that didn't get the bar maid in Kennedy O'Brien's. The next thing all the young lads that would be there waiting for a game were given the door.

It seems some member of the British Legion Club had died and the members came back after the funeral to drink in the club. We were told leave the club, the snooker tables was taken over by this mob of intruders. My rag was truly out and I decided to play a little trick on our intruders. My friend William Dennehy and I went over to O'Connor's Chemist shop in O'Connell St. to use the public phone on the corner of the footpath.

I picked up the phone and dialled 999 asked for the fire brigade and told them there was a fire in the British Legion hall in Hartstonege St. We casually walked back and waited for the excitement to start. I manage to be sitting on the bars out side the club when the fire engine came screaming down the street with bells ringing and pulled up outside the British Legion door. Old Mattie the caretaker opened the door and roared for everyone to get out, he didn't have a clue where the fire was but shouted for everyone to get out. I can still see the surprised look on their faces as the scrambled out the door clutching pints of Guinness in their hands.

When it was realised that it was a bogus call they retreated back into the hall. But I felt great for giving those pricks a small bit of a scare, and I felt pretty good with myself. Six weeks after that a detective sergeant Michael Murphy, a Kerry man called to my house saying, a guy from Vises Field was after spilling the beans on me and my friend William Dennehy.

I remember being fined £3 but my friend William Dennehy got his name in the paper because he was over sixteen years of age. I was saved that embarrassment. It seems a house was burnt to the ground in the city when the fire brigade were sent out on my bogus call. Naturally I felt sorry for what I had done when I heard that.

Kennedy O'Brien's is under new management now, the man that owns it is called Liam Breen for some reason he seems to have the nick name "Happy"; this guy has made huge improvements since it was bought from Joe Mallon. His brother Brendan is the owner of the Windmill Bar that I wrote about in another chapter. Both of those public houses are a pleasure to go into, I remember meeting a friend in Kennedy O'Brien's one Sunday morning. I happened to get in before my friend and when he arrived he stopped to look at what was on offer on the drinks price list in the porch outside.

Finally when he came in I called for his usual drink, which was a small Power Whiskey and a jug of water. My friend then said to me, "How much is a small power here". "Happy", served us and said to my friend, "What were you looking at the price list for". My friend said to him "I'm entitled to look at the price list aren't I, I presume that's why it's hanging outside for people to look at, isn't it?

Happy went on to say he was after spending a fortune on doing the place up, he was going on about how much his insurance was after going up, and paying staff and he said all his prices were too low. My friend looked at Happy and said, "I only came in to have a drink with Austin, not to hear your troubles". Happy said "Whose Austin". My friend said, "You're just after serving him, he bought the drink for me". Happy said, "Oh I'm sorry I thought you were a health inspector checking up on me".

I looked at my friend Denis, and he looked at me, and we both looked at Happy, and we all knew this conversation should not be happening. Talk of a mix up we had another couple of drinks, and headed off to our local public house South's for our usual Sunday morning drink.

We left Happy brooding over the stupid conversation we just had, and we wondered was there anymore guys like us in this crazy world. Credit must be given to Liam Breen and his brother Brendan for the terrific improvements they have carried out to their two public houses, namely Kennedy O'Brien's in Hartstonege St. and The Windmill Bar in Henry St. It's a pleasure to visit anyone of them.

THE END